Life of My Life

A Novel

Vincent Cardinale

Writers Club Press

San Jose New York Lincoln Shanghai

Life of My Life
A Novel

Published by Writers Club Press
an imprint of iUniverse.com, Inc.

For information address:
iUniverse.com, Inc.
620 North 48th Street
Suite 201
Lincoln, NE 68504-3467
www.iuniverse.com

ISBN: 0-595-00627-2

For Marie, Morgan, and Vincent Peter

To the memory of my father,
Vincent Paul Cardinale, Sr.
1914-1983
Butcher

Acknowledgements

To Robin and Fede

Without your generosity and help with the translations of the poems, this book would not have been possible.

Grazie Mille!

Epigraph

Amor Vincit Omnia
Love Conquers Everything

ONE

Everything began to unravel when he stepped from the cold-storage with a hindquarter of beef balanced on his right shoulder and a cloud of frozen air swirling at his feet. He steadied the meat with his right hand and turned and latched the door with his left. He extended his left arm out from his side for balance, paused a moment to thank the beef for cooling him off on this blistering Oakland day, then looked, as he always did at this point, to the front of the shop, towards the counter, to see if any customers needed help. There, surrounded in a heavenly and luminous aurora, stood the most eloquent expression of flesh God's good hand had ever fashioned. The supple arms and tender fingers. The black and braided hair. Eyes so green the Napa Valley foothills must have gone yellow from envy. *Donna valente*, he thought. Rare woman. For two seconds—though not even he knew it—Salvator Cavriaghi's heart stopped beating and his lungs, suddenly filled with her sweet scent, refused to exhale. This is when the beef began to slip. He thought: I must act, I must try to save this meat from falling; I don't want to lose it. So, risking pulled back-muscles, a sprained wrist, even a bruised tailbone, Salvator Cavriaghi, his feet jerking like a tap dancer's, heaved and grunted and wiggled and manipulated his grip, until, by some monumental failure of finesse and speed-prayer, he managed to catapult the hindquarter of beef *under* his butcher's block in just enough time to fling his arms backwards and minimize the embarrassment of his fall. The meat hit the floor with a loud thwack! and, slick with fat and frost, slid under and past his block and crashed into the legs, eight feet away, of his father's old roll-top desk.

Salvator closed his eyes for one second, shook his head, stood, pulled in a breath and held it. Love, armed in a full battle sun dress, pearl skin, and—God help him—perky breasts, had just entered the store and acted. He exhaled, flicked his hands down the front of his smock, then glanced over towards his father's other two employees. Paulo was already laughing and shaking his head, downright sinister; Nino was on his way over to offer some help. And his father? Claudio Cavriaghi did not turn around. Salvator could tell by the tightening of his father's neck, the way it cinched up like a yanked knot, that Claudio's level of happiness had just plummeted from its usual plateau of endearing old-fart grumpiness to a widening valley of genuine anger. Claudio wrapped the girl's five pounds of ground sirloin in a paper trough and white butcher paper and handed her the meat. He waved his hand to say "no" when she handed him the money. Then, in a move never before seen in Cavriaghi's Meats, Claudio Cavriaghi acted with a hint of malice towards a customer: he pointed to the door and said, "Just get out."

In the ten years since Salvator Cavriaghi had been a full-fledged butcher he had never dropped a piece of meat. Never. To do that would violate his father's unspoken promises to his customers: every customer shall be treated with dignity and respect; every customer shall have beautiful, pristine meat. In one day, and in less than two minutes, a singular woman of incomprehensible beauty had precipitated the collapse of these two sacred commandments.

But how unusual all this mishap!

Local myth had it that cattle would gather at night in central Californian pastures, under cloudy, half-moonlit skies, and discuss, at great length, and with deep philosophical conviction, how rich an honor it would be to have the Great Salvator carve them. "Oh," the steers would say, steam puffing through their nostrils, "to be his top sirloin!" Everyone knew that Salvator Cavriaghi said a small prayer over every carcass, and those prayers, according to the myth, were whispered with such pure and honest admiration for life that they actually got livestock into heaven. He prayed for the soul of the animal—he believed all animals had souls—that it was happy. He prayed for himself, that he would carve the flesh with love and fine precision, as though God Himself had commissioned Salvator to prepare a meal for His table. He prayed for the people who would consume the meat, that they would know the beast had given up life for them.

Salvator looked at his father, who had come over to him. "Who was that?" Salvator said, his mind cloudy, as if the beef he'd dropped had landed on his head. Nino went back to the front of the shop. He was a thin, rangy man, this Salvator Cavriaghi, strong though, and just twenty-three years old, with black hair—this is how his mother, Rose, described it—"so long you look like a girl." In truth, only his bangs were long—they'd hang down to his chin if he didn't keep them slicked back with goop—and you could see the mole on the back of his neck even when he wore a collared shirt. He worked with his father and two other men, Nino Di Lampedusa, who Salvator liked to call "Uncle Nino" even though they had no blood between them, and Paulo Bruno, who was only a few years older than Salvator. Together the men cut meat in the small shop on the corner of 49th street and Telegraph, a few miles from Oakland's downtown.

Salvator studied Claudio's aging face, the wrinkles marbled in his skin like the fat in a good porterhouse. It was inevitable Claudio's skills as a butcher would manifest themselves in Salvator, inevitable that the double-helix of Salvator's DNA looked more like two butchered steers held together by chicken neck rungs rather than the more common "twisted ladder" configuration found in other mortals. The entire line of Cavriaghi males, back into the 1500s, had been meat cutters, and before that, farmers, and every single one of them and all of their slaughtered pigs and cattle and chickens were represented in the deep furrows carved into Claudio's face, the same corrugations faintly eroding, Salvator knew, into his own face. Salvator's paternal grandfather, Claudio Sr., there, the deep, deep creases at the edges of Claudio's eyes; his great-uncles Giovanni and Ugo there on his father's face as two deep lines running from the sides of his nose to the edges of his mouth, cavernous; his great-great-grandfather, only visible when Claudio smiled—Iacopone was not visible right now; all the cousins and uncles and grandfathers in their various degrees, all the steers and chickens and pigs, there on his father's face, mapped out in the unalterable fat of history.

"Dad?" Salvator said.

Claudio slid his black-framed glasses down to the end of his nose, then, with his hands, Claudio took up Salvator's hands, palms down. He turned Salvator's hands over a few times, brought them close to his face and rubbed them with his thumbs, then he inspected them slowly, running the tips of his fingers over the backs of his son's hands as methodically as if he were sifting through a pile of white sand for one particular grain. Salvator tried pulling his hands away, not at all interested in this display of paternal concern, worried that if he didn't get out the door within the next two seconds she'd be gone forever; but Claudio, his lips pursed, his face severe, clamped down on his son's hands and continued his systematic inspection—not once looking up into Salvator's eyes—until he'd examined the backs and palms of both of Salvator's hands. A butcher's hands must be kept strong and agile. Any trauma not immediately attended to could ruin future generations of steaks.

"Who was that, Dad?" Salvator repeated.

All of Salvator's ancestors had raised their own cattle, slaughtered it with their own hands, and sold it to support their families. Salvator knew how important it was to his father that he, Salvator, be a butcher. He knew very well the story of his father's parents, how they'd lost fourteen of their twenty-one acres to the government, who, citing "eminent domain," decided the front two thirds of Claudio Sr.'s property, which included the house, was a perfect place to put the new Contra Costa County court house. This was when Salvator's family—his father then only a young boy—moved from Pittsburgh to Monterey. Claudio Sr. opened a shop in Monterey and stayed there until he died, thirty-two years later. Just before his death, Monterey began to develop, malignant buildings sprouting up here and there like sores around a sick person's lips. A few weeks before he died, lying in his bed, the cancer having spread from his colon to other vital organs, Claudio Sr. told Claudio Jr. that he wanted the business to keep going, but that Claudio Jr. should move. "Take the business to Oakland, where they've already paved over everything," Claudio Sr. had said, tired, nearly out of breath. "And have a boy. You need a boy, Claudio."

Claudio finally let go of Salvator's hands. Now he looked Salvator in the eye and said, "That was nobody you need to think about," and turned around and went back to the counter.

Claudio Cavriaghi, himself a crackerjack butcher, had resigned his unofficial title as "Oakland's Best Butcher" six years earlier when other butchers started visiting Cavriaghi's Meats and comparing his son's work with meat to Leonardo Da Vinci's work with oil-based paint. "He is a prophet of meat," the butchers would say, standing around Salvator's cutting block after hours, slack-jawed, pointing with stumped midfingers and arthritic pinkies as Salvator carved out beautifully sliced T-bones. "And so young!" Once, three butchers from Palermo, having heard of a "young butcher in California that makes us all look like we've been playing with dolls for the last ten years," made the trip to Oakland to watch Salvator cut meat. They immediately offered to pay his way to Sicily to teach them and their sons how to cut meat. He respectfully declined. Sicilian butchers, when confronted with a genius artist like a Da Vinci or a Salvator, have no recourse but to obey their bones and concede that the great artist is indeed greater than they. This, of course, does not preclude them from bickering back and forth about who amongst themselves is the *second* greatest butcher. "Claudio," the butchers would say, "your son has surpassed you." And Claudio would smile, knowing they only spoke the truth. What else can a man be but proud when other butchers call his son the greatest butcher since Giacomo Tasso, the legendary beefologist born and raised in Etna, Sicily, who could, among other things, sharpen a knife with one hand while parsing a rump with the other? Salvator coaxed meat into strips and chunks with the same tenderness and concentration great poets give their lines and stanzas. His hands moved over sides of beef like butterflies near the mouths of flowers. Salvator Cavriaghi considered each cut of meat a poem, an artful dance, the spirited language of meat.

It was his mother who had told Salvator, nearly fourteen years ago, that if he wanted meat cutting to be his true art—which he did—he'd need a secondary art to feed the meat cutting and use as an outlet. An excellent piano player capable of playing extremely well in many styles, from classical to jazz to blues, Rose occasionally gave lessons to young children from her church, so she of course wanted Salvator to play piano, but, after a year of his not practicing and being completely incapable of playing even the simplest tune with the slightest hint of passion, she gave up. Then one day, as she was vacuuming the living room, she thought she'd heard one of her old Caruso records playing but couldn't remember having put one on. She turned off the vacuum, and, as she left the living room to go to her bedroom where she kept the record player, she passed the bathroom. It was not a record. It was Salvator, in the bathroom. He was maybe ten years old.

"Salvator?" she'd said.

He stopped singing.

"What are you doing?"

"Taking a dump."

"I mean with the singing. Was that you singing just now?"

Salvator grunted. Grunted again. "Huh?"

Rose raised her voice, "Was that you singing?"

He answered, operatic, "Yes," his voice drawing out the "ess" sound, arpeggiated, making it rise and fall as a leaf would, caught on a breeze.

By the time he was sixteen they were serenading the entire family before, during, and after every Christmas, Easter, and Thanksgiving dinner, she on the piano, he singing opera or Italian folk songs. He loved to take old Italian love poems, memorize them in the Italian, then sing them as if they'd been written for song. The lilt and timbre of the old Sicilian line had seduced Salvator. Poets like Giacomino Pugliese wove lines of such grand romantic magnitude Salvator had no choice but to sing them to himself as he cut meat. Indeed, sometimes he'd become so entranced by a poem's rhythm as he carved meat that the poem itself would become the prayer he recited over the beef, Salvator's link to the Divine. Lines like Umberto Calvino's,

> *Tu entri, io sto fermo*
> *sperando che tu noti, vedi,*
> *allunghi, prendi*
> *con le tue mani delicate*
> *la mia anima*

> you enter, I stand still—
> hoping you notice, see,
> reach out, catch
> with your gentle hand
> my soul

—lines like these, softly sung at the time Salvator sliced meat, could produce steaks so devastatingly fine no other butcher would even bother hoping to approach them in beauty or precision.

Salvator shifted his attention from his father. "Nino?" he said, hoping his surrogate uncle would know the name of the Madonna whose presence had just graced their shop. Nino Di Lampedusa had started working for Claudio three months after Claudio opened Cavriaghi's Meats twenty-four years ago. Their families had known each other since the grandparents had emigrated from Sicily back near the turn of the century. When Claudio decided to leave Monterey and move up to Oakland, he let Nino know that if he ever needed a job, Claudio Cavriaghi would give him one.

Never one to turn down honest work, Nino Di Lampedusa packed his bags two months after Claudio left, asked his girlfriend, Maria Petrocelli, to marry him, and when she didn't, moved north on his own.

Nino, whose face looked like a weathered chunk of redwood burl, peeked up from the front of the glass display case, which he was cleaning, and which he could barely peer over, wiped the sweat from his brow with his forearm, and, waving his hands in the air, said, "Don't ask me! If he ain't talking"—Nino nodded towards Claudio—"I sure in the hell ain't talking."

Oh, it was true Salvator Cavriaghi could cut meat as no one had before him. It was even true he would sing love poems to the female customers while packaging their orders (some of them blushed; others giggled; most rolled their eyes and sighed). But nothing, not even the luscious perfection of a Salvator Cavriaghi veal cutlet could compare in artful significance to the way he sharpened a knife. No doubt his steaks had turned a few lost vegetarian souls into carnivores, a couple of renegade macrobiotics into starving hound dogs, but were it not for his knives and the way he sharpened them, his meat would amount to nothing more than mere maggot grub. At least in his humble opinion. It was as if each blade stroked across his well worn whet stone was being sharpened for use by the Muses. Even old, shriveled butchers, butchers with significant and honorable histories, on errands from their own shops in Pittsburgh, and Hayward, and Monterey, would stop in to watch Salvator sharpen his knives. "Salvator," they would say, "how exactly are you holding your knife? Are you using a light touch today?" or, "At what angle do you drag the blade of a trimming knife after you've sliced up a shank?" or, more often than these, though this usually in a whisper fat with humility: "Salvator, I have only one knife with me today. If you have a minute?" Then the butcher, someone like the prehistoric and highly esteemed Guido Stampa, famous more for his ability to barbecue a chicken than to debone one—he'd poked an eye out back in the '30s—would pull a knife from the back pocket of his exhausted black work pants and hand the knife to Salvator who would then unwrap the knife from its makeshift butcher-paper sheath and commence to sharpening. Often Salvator would set up two stones side by side on his block, then, smiling, perhaps humming some lines from Dino Campana's poem, "The Evening of the Fair," as he did it, Salvator would guide any butcher that asked through the exact steps he took. First: clear your mind of all negative thoughts. Second: allow your heart to fill with beauty. Third: say a small prayer of your own design, no longer than ten words. Fourth: create in your mind an image of your knife as the sharpest knife in the world. Fifth: grip the knife with a compassionate and loving hand and invite the edge of the blade to attain its ultimate sharpness. Sixth: quickly review steps one through five and assure yourself you've completed them with authentic sincerity. You must be perfectly honest here, otherwise the next step will not bring you sharpness. Seventh: sharpen the knife. He would even let other butchers practice with his knives and his stone and his steel. Some believed these blessed by God, and simply to touch them…oh! to touch them!

Nino spoke again: "And Sal, whatever you do"—Nino pointed his crooked index finger at Paulo—"don't listen to this cur."

Fifteen feet and three cutting blocks away from Salvator, Paulo "Schnazzola" Bruno sprinkled salt on half a lemon then rubbed the lemon along the blade of his trimming knife, removing the dried blood and meat. Paulo's smock, a smear of meat drippings, knife smudges, and juice splashings, was looped around his back and tied in the front. Paulo had been working for Claudio ever since graduating from high school nine years ago. Originally, Paulo planned to work only one summer, just long enough to buy a '67 Corvette he'd had his eye on, fill its tank, and head off to college. But Claudio paid him well, so well, in fact, that one summer turned into one year, which turned into two years, which turned into college? What college? and now, as he neared his twenty-eighth birthday, Paulo Bruno had a hot-rodding candy-apple red '67 'Vette with twelve-thousand dollars worth of engine, drive-train, and diamond-tuck interior work, three credit cards, a rent payment for a two bedroom apartment on

Oakland's Lake Merritt, and a special expense account for all the women
willing to go out with him.

Paulo had taut, vibrant skin; lean and powerful muscle. By no means
did he look bulky, like a weight-lifter or body builder. He just looked fit.
What he lacked in height and weight he made up for in speed, agility, and
reflex. And simple grace. Every move Paulo Bruno's body made seemed to
take on the relaxed fluidity of water flowing over slippery river rock. It was
something he worked very hard at every single day. He lived the life of a
dedicated martial artist. His art, ninjutsu, was his life way, and he loved to
talk about it whenever someone else brought it up in conversation. Just
last week he'd returned from what he called a "Tai Kai" in San Diego
where his teacher—or Sensei, as Paulo called him—had presented Paulo
with his second degree black belt. "Hey Nino," Paulo said, his nasally
voice that of a man perpetually trying to catch and sustain a full breath,
"you think Sal here's going to marry that Toscana?"

Claudio walked over to Paulo and smacked him in the ear. "You jackass," Claudio said. Paulo smiled and giggled to himself. If Paulo Bruno was
famous for anything, he was famous for his ability to annoy the crap out of
Claudio Cavriaghi, Salvator Cavriaghi, and Nino Di Lampedusa in less
time than it took those men to properly pronounce their own names. Paulo
had single-handedly—or so it seemed—transformed the age old sports of
bullshitting and friend razzing into high art. Why did Claudio put up with
Paulo? Simple: after himself, Claudio Cavriaghi new no one, not Salvator,
not Nino, not anybody, that could work as hard and for as long, without
any complaint, as Paulo Bruno. And there wasn't anything Claudio
Cavriaghi could say better about a man than that he was a hard worker.

"*That's* Anna Toscana?" Salvator said. "As in Dr. Toscana's daughter?"

Claudio thought for a moment. Then: "Yes. The doctor's daughter."
He nodded his head. "She's off limits." He waved his hands, intense, like
a baseball ump signaling safe: "Period." Claudio pointed his finger at
Paulo and, through clenched teeth, said, "You keep your mouth shut, you
little shit."

Paulo smiled even more broadly. "He's already in love, Claudio. You're screwed." He actually cackled at this one.

L'amore parla di te

Salvator thought, remembering a line from Carmelo Masino

>*'Che bella,' lei dice.*
>*'Che pura,' lei dice.*
>*'Immortale,' lei dice.*

>Love speaks of you:
>'So beautiful,' she says.
>'So pure,' she says.
>'Immortal,' she says.

He remembered the outline of her body, its slender contours, the graceful movements. Was that her voice he'd heard, or the soft and beautiful coo of a dove? Why had he never seen her before? Toscana spoke of her often, how his little Anna just got an "A" on her big research paper, how his precious little Anna will go to Stanford, too, just like her father and mother, how, "if she plays her cards right," she will have her own medical practice by the time she's thirty.

On the sidewalk in front of the shop, a little chubby boy, smiling a wicked little smile, launched a suction-cup arrow at the plate glass window. Salvator started, as if the arrow were on its way in to his chest. He said aloud:

>*Gli angeli ridono!*
>*I bicchieri di cristallo brindano*
>*il suono. Si spegne,*
>*una freccia attraverso il mio cuore*

Angel laugh!
Crystal glasses toast
the sound. It falls,
an arrow through my heart.

For a moment it looked like Claudio's head would burst from the blood
pressure. "Paulo," he said. "I'm going kill you."

Now Paulo laughed out loud.

Nino said: "Don't let him get to you Claude. Just look at that mountain of nose on him." Nino paused. "He bugs you, just look at the nose.
You can't but feel sorry for it, being so big and connected to such an ass
of a face."

Paulo smiled and went back to rubbing his knife. He mumbled something about big noses, then pointed to his crotch.

Salvator wagged a thumb in Paulo's direction. "It never ceases to amaze
me, Nino, that there is enough air left for us to breathe." Anna Toscana
my beautiful, beautiful love. *O donna mia, donna mia.* O my lady, my
lady. My beautiful mocha fudge. My sweet little butterfly.

Salvator removed a sharpening stone from the right drawer of the old
roll-top business desk. Across the top of the desk, strewn about like scattered confetti, stuffed in its cubbyholes like forgotten homework in a boy's
pocket, protruding from its other drawers like tongues, were bills and
notices and other sundry slips of paper. He bent down and pulled the
hindquarter of beef out from under the desk, carried it to his block, then
cleaned it off with a moist cloth. He'd been coming to the butcher shop
nearly since the day he was born. Even during those early days Claudio
impressed upon him the importance of maintaining the integrity of the
Cavriaghi name: "though progress has stolen all of our land," Claudio
would say, "and most of our rituals, we cannot allow it to kill us."
Salvator's grandfather was the last private butcher in California to raise
and slaughter his own beef and sell it in his own shop. And Claudio was
the last butcher in the Cavriaghi line to slaughter by hand. Salvator had

never done it, and never would. The opportunity was simply gone. They just couldn't afford the land.

Salvator withdrew his boning knife from the aluminum sheath on his hip and placed it with the sharpening stone on the shelf next to his block. He went to the sink and saturated his shop towel with water, wrung out the towel, then folded it into quarters and set it on the block. He placed the stone on top of the towel to prevent it from slipping along the block. Salvator Cavriaghi, consciously conjuring the willowy image of Anna Toscana, began to sharpen a knife. Such glorious inspiration! He started by clearing his mind of all negative thoughts, then filling it with Anna's image. He said the following prayer: "God, grant me the strength to endure my father," then pictured his knife as the sharpest knife in the world. He took up the boning knife's smooth wooden handle firmly in his right hand and quickly reassured himself that his intentions were genuine. The fore-and middle-finger and thumb of his left hand then applied pressure to the side of the blade, and he pulled, at an angle, the edge of the knife along the length of the stone, sliding it from the heel of the blade to the point. He repeated the same maneuver to each side of the blade eight times. With sure quickness, he steeled the edge of the blade, sending a fine metallic ring through the shop. He drew the fat of his thumb across the edge of the blade and heard the crisp scrape of flesh that meant the knife was perfect. His thumb had memorized the feeling of a sharp knife; his thumb knew when a knife could fall through meat, rather than be tugged through it. He set the knife on the block and returned the steel to its loop on his belt. He pulled in a deep breath through his nose, held it a moment, then let it out through his mouth. Today was a very good day.

He looked out front, beyond the plate glass windows that formed the front of the store. Waves of light warped in the heat. It was August, and not even any of the old-timers could remember heat like this. A car had overheated right in front of the shop, its owner standing over the steaming engine, shaking his head. He could hear the loud jack-hammering of the city workers repaving the street; the putrid odor of hot asphalt made the

✝

day's heat seem twenty degrees hotter. Across the street: an old man sitting on the curb, depleted, dabbing his head with a handkerchief; behind the man, an even older woman, wearing bright-red skin-tight hot-pants and twirling a heavy, orange umbrella—she was skinny, this one, and infinitely wrinkled, as if years ago, maybe in her forties, she'd been fat, and now all the excess skin hung on her body like old, dry curtains; a young couple, both in sandals, both in tank tops, both in shorts, entered the shop, looked confused, said, "Wrong store," then left.

Three ceiling fans whirred above the men. On the counter next to the cash register, a transistor radio crackled out the weather report: "...ninety-five degrees at three minutes past noon. Looks like President and Mrs. Clinton better wear shorts and tank tops to Chelsea's first day at Stanford tomorrow. They, and everyone else down there in the South Bay, will see it break a hundred before noon..."

"Holy Mama," Paulo said. He lifted his eyebrows and rolled his eyes. "Has it ever been so hot? The paint on my car must be melting."

"Ack," Nino said, flicking his hand in Paulo's direction, "you and that lump of a car. You think women will forgive the nose for the car?" Nino tossed his glass-cleaning rag into a bucket and reached for his broom. He started sweeping under the display case and flicking the dirt towards the center of the floor. Already, at fifty-five, his hands looked like ancient cutting boards, chipped and cracked. His wife, Esme, left him a year ago—after fifteen years of marriage—for a young college man she'd seduced in a bar. The guy's parents were supposedly worth millions. But Nino knew why she'd left. Like he'd said to Salvator: "Ain't got nothing to do with money and everything to do with this fat ass beer gut." After three months of bawling and heavy drinking, Nino Di Lampedusa had resigned himself to the knowledge that his wife was gone, and that he needed to start working on himself, both physically and mentally, if he ever wanted to have another relationship with a woman. He'd lost thirty-six pounds in the last six months—you could hardly tell he'd had a formidable belly just twelve months earlier—and he'd quit drinking. The truth was, ever since Esme left him, he'd never felt better. Other women had started to notice him. One in particular, Becky Shaw, a business woman almost a foot taller than Nino, with enormous brown eyes and thin, wire-rimmed glasses, would come in to the shop just to talk with Nino. "Good thing that woman left you," she'd said once, noticeably staring at his mid-section. This Nino loved. He bent down and swept the pile of dirt into the dustpan. "Be glad you work in here," Nino said to Paulo, "if you call that work, you shrimp. Those men out there, paving the street, see 'em?, how they do that in this heat I'll never know."

"Oakland sweats like a damn farm animal," Paulo said. "Goddamn farm animal." Paulo wiped his nose on his right shoulder.

Salvator returned his attention to the meat. He rested the thin tips of his fingers on the edge of the block, closed his eyes, then lifted his chin and inhaled deeply through his nose. He kept his tie—always a black one—cinched up at his throat and tucked into his shirt just below the first button. He wanted to smell the thin white layer of fat that coated the meat, taste first in his nostrils the thickness of the bull's life and blood. This took concentration. He had to ignore the faint smell of the honing oil and whet stone at the edge of the block, ignore the powerful odor of Paulo's fresh cut lemons, ignore the acrid stench of hot asphalt permeating the entire city; he had to ignore the lingering fragrance of Anna Toscana.

Of them all, it was this last one, that voluptuous mix of peppermint and basil, that his heart, pounding as if he had just sprinted a mile, could no longer overlook.

TWO

By ten minutes after six, Nino, Paulo, and Claudio had left for home, and Salvator Cavriaghi was alone in the shop. The construction on the street outside had not yet stopped—they'd work under artificial light until nine at night—and traffic outside was swelling, "clotting" Nino liked to say. And the traffic would stay thick, like blood on its way to the heart, until well after seven. Between customers and phone calls and a trip to the bank, Salvator hadn't gotten to the hindquarter that had almost killed him earlier in the day. But now, with the store empty, Salvator could take his time and slice the meat as it should be sliced: slowly, and with care. He brought the beef back out to his block, this time easily lifting it to his shoulder without the slightest hint of imbalance. With smooth and deliberate strokes, Salvator parsed the waiting hindquarter into three sections: the rump, the loin, and the top hindquarter. He removed the top and loin back to cold storage and set to carving the rump section. What a rump on that Anna Toscana, Salvator thought.

He found the leg bone on the inner side of the shank and ran his boning knife along that seam, releasing the main portion of the shank from the leg. I'm carving a rump. "Anna Toscana," he said aloud. Her rump, her green eyes, everything so beautiful! Salvator sliced through the remaining fat and sinew connecting the meat to the bone and completely separated the piece of meat from the rump section. Such a beautiful rump, he thought. So round and firm. So smooth. He hefted it in both hands. Oh Anna. He returned the remaining portion of the rump back to the cold room. After removing the excess fat with his carving knife, Salvator cubed the meat, wrapped it in white butcher paper—he threw in an extra quarter pound for free—and labeled it with Mr. Fante's name. He took the package up to the refrigerated meat counter and carefully placed it in the far right corner next to the sliced salami. Claudio Cavriaghi was one of the first butcher's in California to not only make his own salami—Salvator would, upon Claudio's retirement, become the Cavriaghi Salami Executor—but sell it, and cooked ham and turkey in his shop. "Salvator," his father had told him once, "if you can get them in to the shop to buy a sandwich, you can get them to leave the shop with a sandwich *and* a steak."

The phone rang, a good, loud, genuine ringing, not the electronic whistle you get so much of these days. As far as Salvator knew, they were the only business on the avenue who still used a rotary telephone.

"I will be home, probably seven o'clock," Salvator said into the phone.

His mother, Rose, at the other end of the line: "We're out of chuck, and I wanted to cook some tomorrow, with potatoes. Your father was supposed to bring it."

"How much you want?"

"Couple pounds," Rose said, her voice distant, as if the mouthpiece of the phone were up around her forehead, which it probably was. Salvator pictured Rose with her head cocked to one side, the phone pinched between her ear and shoulder, both her hands plunged into the bowl of ground round—if she's calling about tomorrow's dinner, she must be making tonight's, he thought—kneading the raw meatloaf with her fist, then squeezing it between her fingers, fully mixing in the bread crumbs, the parsley, the couple of eggs, the parmesan cheese, the dash of Italian seasoning, the sprinkle of black pepper, the little bit of ketchup.

"I'll bring it with me tonight," Salvator said. "And I'll stop and pick up some sourdough, too."

✝

Salvator smiled and nodded. Four years ago, at his own sixtieth birth-day party, Claudio Cavriaghi secured the future of his and his father's craft by handing the keys to Cavriaghi's Meats over to Salvator.

"I'll be leaving at five o'clock from now on," Claudio had said, holding up a glassful of cabernet in Salvator's direction, "and you might as well get used to closing up the shop now"—he gulped some wine—"since it's going to be yours in five more years."

Salvator beamed at the unexpected gesture, as if his father hadn't handed over the keys to a building on Telegraph Avenue, but the future to a legacy of men.

In the intervening four years since passing the keys to his son, Claudio had slowly distanced himself from the day to day running of the business, even once going so far as to take an entire day off. Though Claudio still managed the money, Salvator was now in charge of placing orders, of opening and closing the shop, of deciding what would go where in the meat counter. And what a job Salvator had done on the meat counter! From left to right, the display case was packed with meat. A customer's mouth would water at the sight of it! Ground sirloin, ground chuck, and ground round. Cubed stew meats, whole steaks, and stuffed pork chops. Whole chickens, half chickens, deboned chickens. Chicken sliced in strips, chicken trimmed to breasts and thighs, chicken necks for soup. Rolls of hot sausage and mild sausage, homemade salami, and mortadella. Lamb chops and T-bones, bottom steaks and beautiful hams, sandwich steaks, hamburger steaks, and filet mignon.

Salvator fiddled with some papers on the desk. To his left: Nino's block, then his, then Paulo's, then his father's, the end of the display case, the western wall of the store, and, beyond the wall, 49th street, then a small parking lot and a bank. To his right: the eastern wall of the store, brick, with arched windows now boarded up and plastered over. On the other side of the wall, an empty store. Empty for two years now. Then another empty store, this one smaller than the first. Then Polaski's Hardware. Then a pawn-shop, a small restaurant, and, finally, on the corner of 51st and Telegraph, a check-cashing store. In front of Salvator: the display case, the front of the store, and the mighty Telegraph Avenue pumping people to and from Oakland's downtown. Behind him: the back wall of the store, the cold storage, the little parking lot, then homes and apartments, then, half a mile later, Broadway, Telegraph's twin sister.

My mother, Salvator thought, returning to his block. "Rose Cavriaghi," he said aloud, as he often did, shaking his head. What a woman. She is my mother, and she is going to school. She is my I-will-have-dinner-ready-and-waiting-while-I'm-off-to-school mother. She will have the house clean. She will have the clothes washed and dried and put away. She is my mother, he thought. My mother. Twenty-three years! My mother who took me to school and picked me up. Every morning, for two years now, you do your meditation thing, what's it called? You used to smile everyday, Mom. Rose with lines in her lovely face and blackness under her tired eyes. "Take a vacation, Claudio." I've heard you say that. "A week, just you and me," you tell him, "a week alone." Has he taken a week? No. He's only taken a day, and on that day he sat in his chair and watched television.

Of course, no one, especially Rose Cavriaghi, would ever deny Claudio his rest. He'd certainly earned it, having built up a business that had thrived so well for over a quarter of a century that Rose never had to get a job, never had to worry about money or bills. Salvator was willing to give his father that much. But Salvator couldn't excuse his father for the lack of attention he, Claudio, paid Rose. Salvator believed—and the older he got the more strongly he believed it—that though hard work may be one of the elemental components that makes up a man, it's not worth spending twelve to fifteen hours a day in a tiny shop, every day, for *decades*, if it means the remaining hours of each day are spent sleeping rather than playing with the family.

But who was Salvator to talk? He was headed right down the same path his father had paved. Claudio would retire completely by the end of the next year and at that time, like it or not, the future of Cavriaghi's Meats would be resting firmly in Salvator's lap. Claudio Cavriaghi had built a strong clientele, and Salvator certainly felt the pressure to not only keep that clientele strong and healthy, but to draw new people to it. Which, as of today, didn't seem like such a tough or terrible job, considering business hadn't been this good in years. Salvator had no idea why things had picked up over the course of the last few months. And neither did his father. Maybe people were just plain hungrier. Maybe it had something to do with the X-rated theater on the next block finally being shut down. But even with these two things factored in, it didn't make sense that Cavriaghi's meats was doing any business at all.

Seven years ago, when the city tore down Vern's Market across the street and left a gaping, rat infested, weed-choked lot, the local business own-ers—Claudio Cavriaghi included—marched down to city hall and demanded something be done with the scab. For nearly half-a-century Vern's had been a popular—and prosperous—locally owned and operated grocery store, but ten years ago, when the Safeway chain moved in a mile up 51st street, business started to slow down, until, like a beached whale, Vern's had no alternative but to die. The city erected a chain link fence around the lot and said they couldn't do much more unless someone wanted to buy the property. A new grocery store chain expressed interest but then backed out when its engineers dug around and discovered that over 120 years earlier the lot housed a trolley car garage and station and that the dirt in the lot had soaked up hundreds of thousands of dollars worth of toxic oil clean-up. The lot became untouchable.

Two years after Vern's came down, the gas station on the corner opposite Cavriaghi's Meats came down, too. Something about moving the station further up town. With those two businesses gone, Claudio and Salvator thought for sure they'd have to quit and close up shop. Those businesses brought in customers. Mac Johannssen closed down his fresh fruit store; he'd invested thirty-two years of his life on the avenue. Bettie Jones shut down her hair boutique; for nineteen years she'd coifed the local women's hair. Even old man Mazurkowicz bailed out; his grandfather had opened the shoe repair shop on the avenue before the turn of the century.

"Unbelievable," Mazurkowicz had said when the gas station closed. Nobody had heard from him since. But Tom Polaski, owner of Polaski Hardware three doors down from Cavriaghi's Meats, reminded Claudio and Salvator that "people may change, places may change, items may change, but you know what? everybody will always need food and hardware. That's a fact." He was right. Of the twelve businesses on the block at the time the gas station closed, only Cavriaghi's Meats and Polaski Hardware remained. Some of the vacated stores eventually filled up, but most of the businesses on the block today swirled in and out of existence like dust storms. Three pawn shops had cycled through, two health food stores, six little coffee houses had come and gone, a pizza-by-the-slice joint lasted about a year and a half.

The latest rumor scurrying around the area was that some super-sized chain store that sold everything from toilets to furniture to refrigerators to the food to keep in the refrigerators was planning to buy up the block across the street. "Urban renewal," one customer said, a slick-haired man with unbelievably white teeth and a grin like a lizard's. "All in the name of progress," another man had said. "Progress towards what?" was all Salvator had thought to say.

Now Salvator went back to the cold storage and removed a few large round steaks. He would need them for tomorrow's sandwich meat. To cut the steaks for sandwiches, he had to thin them to a thickness of approximately one eighth of an inch. To do this, Salvator plopped the steaks on his block, pulled one forward, then, with the heal and palm of his left hand, he flattened the meat, holding it tight against the block so that his right hand could guide the knife through the flesh at the correct depth.

The image of Anna's shoulders suddenly overwhelmed him and his mind swept away the thoughts of his parents and the future of Cavriaghi's Meats and plunged him into a swoon.

> *Divinità e la semplicità*
> *delle tue membra morbide*

✝

he said aloud

> Divinity is the simplicity
> of your soft limbs

His voice lurked at the edge of song. How your hair is like shimmering strands of coal. How I wish we could walk hand-in-hand along San Francisco's wharf, Anna Toscana, holding hands, Anna, watching the sky turn pink and orange, how we could talk for hours about poetry and music while sitting in the park! Let's carve our initials in a bench! Let's walk the beach, and go to the museum. But my father says you're too young, only seventeen.

Now Salvator Cavriaghi started slicing sandwich steaks at a rate unprecedented in Modern Butchery. What's six years? he said. If I was thirty and you were twenty-four, who'd care? And I know my father doesn't think too much of your father. That Arturo Toscana of yours, the big cigar smoking plastic surgeon, and with a fancy Chevrolet. He waved his knife in the air, as if conducting the Spheres, swung it back down to the meat and continued slicing. He was still talking to himself: And my father, just an old-fashioned meat cutter. Wooden.

He was slicing the second steak when someone knocked on the door. He looked up while he was cutting—he could cut meat with his eyes closed—and saw Anna Toscana standing at the door waving in the stiff armed way of a little girl.

She was alone, wearing the same devastating sundress she'd been wearing earlier, the one with the thin straps hanging over her full, milky shoulders. Her hair was down—look at it!—unbraided. Oh God, Salvator thought, her hair is down!

Here she was! Alone! And him alone! Waving. Smiling. In a thin sun dress that made her look like an amaryllis blossom. Alone.

† ——————

Chi sono io adesso?
Non lo so.
Io conosco solamente te.

Who am I anymore?
I do not know.
I know only you.

Salvator, his attention blasted to the heavens, pulled the blade of his trimming knife deep into the palm of his left hand, from the base of the pinky to the butt of the thumb. The cut was half an inch deep, but clean. When he realized what he'd done, Salvator turned from the block, reached with his right hand to untie the smock, swore, swore some more, then wrapped the smock around his hand as tightly as he could. I have cut my hand, he thought. I have finally cut my hand.

Salvator's hand bled as if he'd just slit its throat. He leaned against his block. This is unbelievable, he said to himself. The wound, and his heart, and other places on his body, throbbed. Dad's going to kill me. How do I explain *this*? The whole city seemed to vibrate and shiver as his pride pumped out of his palm, soaked through the smock, and dripped to the floor.

Oh Jesus Christ, he said, shaking his head. He pulled in a deep breath through his nose. Can it get any better than this?

Embarrassed, and a little queasy, he went to the door and unlatched it with his good hand.

"Anna," he said, bowing as if before a great Akkadian princess.

"Hi," she said, smiling. "You know my name?" She nodded as if to say I'd like to come in, but Salvator didn't notice. "I forgot to pick up some pork chops," she said, stepping past him and into the shop. He was too busy closing his eyes and sniffing the sweet, rarefied air, imagining the two of them floating on a fluffy cloud over the city's rooftops, him on one knee singing his wedding proposal to her, she accepting, his hand stitched up like a goon's. She noticed the blood. Her smile vanished. "Your hand!"

The now-useless smock, thoroughly soaked, looked gruesome, like the haphazardly wrapped stump of a war victim. "I'm fine. Fine," Salvator said. He shrugged it off. He summoned the will of God to keep his eyes from her lips, the beacons calling his heart: the tiny slopes he ached to memorize. How he had never felt such temptation in the presence of a woman! Or pain in his limbs. How many beautiful women had come in to the shop since he'd started working there? A thousand? A million? A billion trillion? How many had he sung poetry to? Sliced meat for? It didn't matter. How many women did he see on the street or in stores or at the movies? It didn't matter. Not one of them had done to his soul what Anna Toscana had accomplished simply by standing in the shop. He'd gone to his senior prom with Naomi Wilson, but she had to ask him. Salvator consciously spent his time working on his art. All the spare time he could have spent dating, he spent sharpening knives, or carving one more side of beef, or reading another book on butchery. His testosterone stores were full up and working fine, no slump in activity there. He loved women, all right. He loved the curves of their bodies, the sounds of their voices, the way they simply acted more *elegant*. But he'd always loved cutting meat *more*, and he always believed that when the right time came, the right woman would make herself known.

Anna was standing next to him, scented like a field of basil and peppermint, shimmering like evening rain. The smooth gypsum of her arm brushed his bare bicep. Her breath, like strawberries.

> *Dio in Cielo*
> *lasciami morire qui, adesso,*
> *dove posa il mio cuore,*
> *pulsando.*

God in Heaven,
let me die here, now,
where my heart lies,
beating.

Salvator's face reddened; the cut pumped. Here he was, alone with the only woman he'd ever met that had made his groin twitch and his heart thump—how was that even *possible?*—and he had a self-inflicted wound the size of East Oakland in his palm. For a moment he thought perhaps he should run and get the knife and just plunge it into his heart, though that probably wouldn't even begin to scratch the pain he was going to feel when his father and mother and Paulo and Nino find out about this. He couldn't figure out what would be worse: the pain in his palm, his parents' anger, or the ribbing Paulo and Nino would inflict upon him. By offing himself he wouldn't have to hear any of the "oohs" and "ahhs" of his friends and family and all the butchers and customers who would come to see him or call him and wish him well, or the "finally!" of weasly folks like Marco Sarconi of Sarconi's Meats down in Monterey, son of Angelo Sarconi, who, according to Claudio Cavriaghi, stole Claudio Cavriaghi's linguica recipe. Salvator made a sign of the cross. He shook his head, smiled, and looked at Anna. Unbelievable, he thought to himself. Un. Be. Lievable.

"I think we should go to the hospital," she said. He thought he heard angels singing, harps and triumphant cherubic faces praising the Almighty. "Come on, Salvator,"—my name! she knows my name!—"we're going to the hospital. This thing is bleeding too much. My car is right in front." When she hooked her left arm under his right arm he noticed, near the back of her right tricep, just close enough to her body where someone would have to be at an odd angle to see it, a bruise. A bruise about the size of a thumb.

THREE

The sky had that heated, wavy quality that squishes all sounds into one slow *wumph, wumph*. Salvator leaned further into Anna's side as they exited the shop. She was strong, as if beneath the innocent facade of her lissome figure was the body of an Olympian. He felt—and he didn't know why—the significant absence of birds, as if, in a moment of clarity, he'd realized how the absolute chaos of the avenue must have felt to the winged creatures, how, if he had wings, he would fly away, too, away from the ubiquitous pavement and steel and shimmering glass, the relentless heat. Yes, absolute chaos, he thought. He'd take her hand and fly her away. Amore! For as far as he could see: cars. Cars honking. Cars swerving. Cars pumping out smoke and stink. Cars. And cars. Cars that sounded like old dying men, hawking up their lungs and cussing at their doctors. Sleek cars and bandaged cars; cars that limped and cars that sped. Cars with sirens and cars with blaring horns. All of them spitting and puffing. The scent of bread wafting from the bakery across the street filtered through the caustic rankness of hot asphalt…together, these scents, and the scent of his own blood, now strong to him, made Salvator nauseous.

An ambulance, its siren and horn wailing, tried to slither around the stopped cars, around the asphalt workers, a snake amongst rocks. He sensed the people of Oakland milling around him and felt comfort in the sensing: the Black barbecue ribs up the street at The Soul Brother's Kitchen, the Italian pastas at La Trattoria, the Mexican rices at Supremo Burrito, the Japanese fish over on 52nd, the Indian curry three doors up, the Puerto Rican chickens in the apartment across the street, the Polish sausages, the Chinese vegetables, the French cheeses, the German beers. And these were the people of Oakland, too, all of them, out there, somewhere on the avenue, thrumming to the city's inner rhythm, walking by each other, nodding, exchanging glances, exchanging breath and kisses and anger and love and sadness and passion: the ragged bodies of homeless folks living by their wits and the super-rich mansion dwellers, the high-school kids with no place to go and the expensive country clubbers, the corporateers wolfing down moms and pops, the delivery people and the people receiving deliveries, the college folks looking for work and the displaced workers thinking about going back to college, the police, the firefighters, the crooks, and the arsonists, the hard workers and the panhandlers, the hard-rock rockers and the hip-hop poets.

Salvator reached into his right pocket and withdrew the store keys. "I need you to lock it up," he said, bobbing his head in the direction of the door.

Anna had her father's meticulously maintained, fully restored 1955 Chevrolet Bel-Air 2-door Hard Top. How did Salvator know this was Arturo's car? When Arturo Toscana came into the shop to buy his meat he talked about four things: his money, his car, his wife, or his daughter. On a good day, he could get in something about all four. "I tell you, Claudio," Toscana would say—he always had to have Claudio help him, as if Salvator and Nino and Paulo simply didn't know enough about meat—"I work ten, twelve hours a day"—at a line like this, Nino and Salvator would look at each other and roll their eyes; Paulo would snort—"bring that Marietta home twice as much money as she needs, and she still bitches at me when I go out to work on the '55. What I'm going to do with her I don't know." Always a variation on this theme with Toscana. Salvator never felt at ease around Toscana, as if the man purposely projected a menacing sneer towards people he disliked. And that was definitely part of it: for some reason

Salvator felt Toscana didn't like him. Is it my work? Salvator wondered. Am I just not high enough on the food chain? Once, Toscana down right scared Salvator. Toscana came in to the shop full of rage and fury. A patient had accused him of malpractice and was threatening to go public if he didn't settle. He had Claudio make him a salami sandwich, which Toscana started eating while Claudio gathered the rest of the order. Toscana took nearly half the sandwich in his mouth with the first furious bite, and while he tried to chew he also tried to talk, or yell, really, at Claudio, or at least in Claudio's direction, and while he did this, his face reddened and he spit out chunks of the sandwich all over the front of the display case. Toscana paced back and forth in front of the case, a tiger teased by steak, gesturing with the sandwich, trying to screech curses out of the side of his mouth. Salvator had thought at the time that Toscana might at any moment leap over the display case and take his rage out on Claudio.

Toscana kept every inch of the car polished: the chrome bumpers, the wheel wells, the exhaust pipes, even the antenna's tear-drop tip. The car's two-tone paint—white on top, green on the bottom—was so shiny the local hot-rod parts store had a picture of it on their cash register, some kind of bogus pin-up model. The truth of it was, Toscana did little if any of the work on the car himself. Oh, he cleaned it, changed a spark plug every now and again, even changed the oil with his delicate touch, but by his own admission, he'd hired out for all the major work. He'd had it dipped and stripped, had the frame sandblasted, the floorboards replaced, the deck lid and hood repaired. He'd even admitted to allowing a little fiberglass filler being used on the car's right quarter panel: "Till I find one meets my standards." Everything on the car was stock, from the 265 V8 to the original hood bird, which wasn't exactly original to that particular car since he'd bought it from a New-Old Stock dealer. Arturo bought the car back in '77 from the proverbial old lady who used it to go to church on Sundays. He was the second owner.

Anna opened the passenger door and helped Salvator in. "Just relax," she said. "You'll be fine."

When she slid in next to him, Salvator's eyes fell on the bicep of her right arm. He could have sworn he saw the lingering reddish imprint of four fingers, the remains of a too-tight grip. But he couldn't be sure.

"What's the quickest way to the hospital?" Anna asked.

"Go to the light and make a right," Salvator said. He scanned the traffic. "Get off Telegraph," he said, "or we'll never get there."

Anna nodded and pulled into traffic.

"Don't dent this car!" Salvator said, smiling.

Anna returned his smile. Laughed even. But when she made the right turn at the light, she made it a little too quickly, trying to beat another car coming the opposite way, and Salvator, out of reflex, threw his left hand out to the dash to keep from sliding down the seat. The blood smeared across the main portion of the dash, and before Salvator could right himself, he had, not thinking, pushed down on the seat with his left hand. "Shit," he said, then, embarrassed, "My God Anna, I'm sorry. I'll pay for this." He tried to wipe the blood off with his forearm, but it only smeared.

"Salvator," Anna said, touching his arm, stopping him. "My dad will understand."

Salvator thought: Your dad will think I'm a fly on the turd of life. He smiled and nodded.

Salvator's hand throbbed, and he looked at it periodically, between glimpses out the window and peeks at Anna. Such succulence. Suddenly, in a moment of sheer anarchy and betrayal, his mouth and heart—his reasonable mind could not stop them—mutinied: "You are incredibly beautiful," he said. Then, reason tossed overboard: "Like Venus in the warm night sky, you are beautiful."

She blushed. Momentarily giggled. Checked herself.

Of the store fronts they passed, probably half of them were boarded up or had shattered windows or bullet holes. The other half had what looked like tank-proof iron gates in front of them. Flattened paper bags, crumpled paper cups, greasy dirt. These things lined the gutters. Homeless people slept on some of the bus stop benches, or tried to find shade under the awning of an abandoned building.

Salvator squinted and looked at Anna. She was speeding, concentrating on traffic, looking in her rearview mirrors, sitting forward in her seat, trying to focus her attention on preventing an accident. Her feet reached the pedals on the floorboard just enough to make it safe for her to drive the car. Why *did* she have her father's car? If she noticed him looking at her—how couldn't she?—she did not let on. He couldn't stop marveling at the length of her hair. Was it even legal to display such beauty in public places? How many old men had died seeing that hair? She turned to look at him, and the sun momentarily glinted off her eye, sparkled there for an instant, a singular, distant star, galactic. She had acne, tiny white capped peaks and reddened valleys on her face, and she wore no make-up. An honest woman, he thought, and fell deeper in love.

The shape of her jaw was like that of an athlete's. Strong. Squared at the edges. Had Toscana said once that she was a swimmer? Salvator couldn't remember.

She looked over at him, smiled. "Why do you think I'm beautiful?"

He nodded and stuck out his lower lip. "Oh," he said, tilting his head a bit to the right, then, closing his eyes, his voice took on the soft and muted sound a man employs when wooing a beautiful woman. He began to sing:

> *La sommossa di primavera tace*
> *ha soggezione di te*

> The riot of spring is quieted
> in awe of you

Salvator opened his eyes, slowly, as if waking from a deep, deep sleep. He looked at Anna. Her eyebrows seemed raised, the look of a bored woman.

"Oh," she said. She rolled her eyes. "You're a poet."

Salvator shook his head, wiggled his forefinger in the air. "Not a poet," his head wagged slightly from side to side, "a butcher."

She laughed. He could see the gaps between her teeth, the cock-eyed bicuspid. She liked him, he thought. At least she didn't look frightened.

Salvator looked at the blood drying on the seat and dashboard.

They came to a red light. He looked away from her, out the passenger's window. An enormous, sweating man slept under the shade of a furniture store's awning. Salvator recognized the man. He was the same man that came into the shop every Monday morning at ten a.m. looking for scraps, always wearing the same greasy, oil stained blue down coat (now balled up as a pillow), the same shredded tennis shoes and soiled blue corduroy pants, the same tattered baseball cap. His long, bushy beard, loaded with food particles, concealed his face, which Salvator often thought was the face of a wise man, a wild man, a man who knew too damn much about too damn much, and all this knowing had driven the man crazy. The man stank so bad of piss and sweat that other customers, covering their mouths and noses, would leave the store when he walked in—some never returned. "All I needs," the man would say, "is some food. Just a little foods all I needs." And Claudio would make the man a sandwich. "Next time, you pay!" Claudio would say, feigning anger. There had been a hundred next times. The man never came in more than once a week, if that often. Once, Salvator hadn't seen him for over a month. Worried that the man had died alone somewhere, Claudio—sandwich in hand—had taken two afternoons to look for the man, up and down the avenue, peeking into other stores' entryways, asking one or two of the other store owners if they'd seen him. Then, as if on cue, the man appeared a few days later, stinkier than ever. Had the man given up? Had he just gone on and found food elsewhere? Salvator didn't know. He looked at Anna, took a breath and held it for three seconds, held up his hand, then said, "I have fallen in love with you."

"You're nuts!" But she was blushing again, and smiling. "You've known me for about a total of ten minutes!" She looked out the driver's side window and put on her left blinker. "That's just not possible."

"Believe it," he said. He smiled. "And you love me, too. You just don't know it yet." He nodded his head and raised his eyebrows. "You will," he said.

Old, wrinkled people filled some of the chairs in the hospital waiting room. Most of them were there, it seemed, just to soak up the air-conditioning. A garbled mush of voices: nurses calling names, patients conversing about sports or the heat or government screw-ups. As Salvator's eyes scanned the room, he saw the people of Oakland he knew so well: a young couple cooing over their tiny baby, telling the baby you'll be okay, you'll be okay, the baby screeching, her face red as an apple, a nurse calling them in; another couple: two young women holding hands, whispering in each other's ears, one crying, the other woman kissing her ear, then her lips, hugging her, as if saying everything will be okay, don't worry, another kiss; a young man, maybe sixteen or seventeen, in T-shirt and jeans, a Raiders baseball cap cocked sideways on his head, ignoring his grandmother sitting next to him, his grandmother, her arms crossed over her chest, looking the other way, angry, as if she knew the boy felt burdened by having to take her to the hospital, as if they both knew somebody else had sent them there because they thought grandma needed to see a doctor; more old folks, many of them alone, some in pairs, some fanning themselves with the magazines and brochures scattered about the room, some sleeping; a middle aged man with lamb-chop sideburns, sitting alone, waiting for someone, his face stern and rigid.

The guard at the desk, a powerful looking man, asked Salvator and Anna if they needed to see a doctor. "My friend has cut his hand very badly," Anna said, dragging Salvator by his bicep to the desk. "He's lost a lot of blood. He needs to see a doctor right away."

Salvator held up the bloody hand in the bloody smock.

The guard did not look up from his desk. He was reading something. "You have to fill this out," the guard said, pulling a medical form out from behind his desk. "Then go over to the nurse's window." The guard pointed to a window across the room.

Anna raised her voice. "He's lost a lot of blood. He needs to see a doctor right now!"

The guard nodded, then, as if to say, I know that, he scanned the room, apparently suggesting the obvious: so does everyone else. He looked like the kind of person capable of assessing a situation quickly. Here was a man and woman, one bleeding. The bleeding one isn't rushing around, doesn't look frantic. They have time to fill out a form. The guard tilted his head to the left, "You're Salvator, aren't you? Mr. C's son?"

Salvator nodded.

The guard smiled and nodded. "I used to come in every day when I was in high school," the guard said, "to buy my dad his steak." Salvator looked at the guard more closely, tried to recognize him. "I'm Damon," he said. "'Little Damon', Mr. Johnson's kid."

Salvator nodded. "Damon," Salvator said. "What happened to you? You're huge!" The last time he'd seen Damon, Damon barely looked strong enough to carry the steak out of the store. Now it looked like Damon could lift the side of the building if he didn't feel like using the front door.

Damon smiled again. "It's all that meat your dad sold me." Damon stood, and he and Salvator shook hands. "I graduated three years ago. I started lifting weights, working out in a gym. And, well," he extended his arms to his sides, obviously proud of his accomplishment.

"You look great, man. Whyn't you come in some time and have a sandwich with me? Dad would love to see you."

"I'll do that," Damon said, sitting back down.

†

Salvator bobbed his head in Anna's direction: "This is Anna Toscana," Salvator said. "I'm going to marry her and we are going to have children." Salvator smiled. Anna shook her head and looked at the ceiling. Damon looked at Salvator. Salvator said: "Well, she hasn't agreed to that yet. We just met a few minutes ago."

Damon and Anna exchanged smiles.

Anna pulled Salvator towards the nurse's window. Salvator looked back to Damon and said, "You come in, okay?" Damon nodded, but his attention was already on the man and child who'd just come in the door.

The room was painted white. A thin strip of wood circled the room at about waist-height, off-setting the white monotony. The doors were finished in the same wood-grain color as the moulding. All of the chairs were covered in a light brown vinyl, the kind of stuff that freezes in winter and gets stickier than fly strips in summer. Each wall had one brightly colored print, apparently meant to further break up the monotonous white walls.

Salvator and Anna got to the nurse's window, filled out the paperwork, and waited for Salvator's name to be called. A nurse called him in immediately.

As Salvator stood, Anna said, "I'll go call your dad." For a moment, Salvator thought to say "No, don't bother" but then decided against it. He just nodded, then followed the nurse into the back of the emergency wing.

The nurse seated him on a gurney and instructed him to lay back.

"Cut yourself?" a voice said.

"Yes."

"Doing what?"

"Slicing some meat. I'm a butcher."

The doctor nodded slowly, said, "Hmm." She paused, then said, "My name's Marianne." She unwrapped Salvator's makeshift bandage. "At least it's a clean cut. Must have been a sharp knife."

Salvator bit down on his upper lip and looked away from his hand. "This gonna hurt?" he said.

✝

"A little," the doctor said, "but then you won't feel a thing. I'm going to numb your hand so I can stitch you up."

Salvator jerked a little as the needle went in to his palm, but within seconds the drug started to take effect, and once his hand was numb, all the muscles in his body finally relaxed. He exhaled and closed his eyes as the doctor worked. He'd blown his reputation. He would have been able to cover up the dropping of the meat. But this? A scar? A wound everyone would notice? No. Things had changed. He felt as though he could no longer call himself a butcher, as though everything he'd worked hard for and identified with had poofed away like dust swatted from a ratty old chair. He knew his father's disappoint would be unbearable. And his mom? Who knows what she would think? Sometimes Salvator thought she wished he'd give up cutting meat and do something else, other times he thought she believed he should never give up the art. Whatever. She'd probably like the idea of him dating a girl, though. Not that they were dating. Yet. Rose was the one that always egged him on to sleep with someone. "You need to practice," she'd say. "You're going to get married some day and you need to practice. Besides, it'll help with those pimples." Yes, good chance Mom would like all of this, would like the idea of her son falling from Grace in the name of Love.

"That's it," the doctor said. She laid his hand on his stomach. "No work for at least a few days, okay? If you can go a week, go a week."

"Thank you," Salvator said.

"Just go home and take it easy. Get yourself some ibuprofen for the pain. It'll start hurting again in a few hours."

Salvator nodded and the doctor left the room.

The nurse came back and said, "All done."

By the time Salvator emerged from the back room with his hand wrapped in a clean bandage, Anna was flanked on her left by her father and on her right, a pace or two away, by Salvator's own parents. Anna had her arms crossed. They were all standing. Claudio and Toscana were arguing about the blood stain in the Chevrolet.

Salvator held his hand up in front of his chest. He smiled and walked up to his father, tried to draw their attention.

"Just a small cut," he said as he approached Claudio. "Some stitches. That's all." He leaned over to kiss his father on the cheek.

"How'd you do it?" Claudio asked. He looked strong in his v-neck T-shirt and black gabardines. He smelled of garlic.

"I don't know, really," Salvator said. He thought he felt the dull thud of his pulse deep in the wound's center.

"You fooling around with my daughter?" Arturo Toscana said, raising his voice so everyone in the room could hear him. His face was the shape of a hundred-year-old shovel, and about as pretty. He was about as wide as he was tall. "Because if you're fooling around with my daughter, I'll kill you."

Salvator looked at Toscana's bulbous belly and glistening bald head and thought: I can take him. "She just drove me to the hospital. We didn't have sex in the car."

Toscana flinched forward, as if he were going to charge Salvator. Damon, the guard, stood up and walked over.

"Everything okay Mr. Cavriaghi? Dr. Toscana?"

Claudio nodded. "Nothing to worry about, Damon. We're fine."

Damon looked Toscana in the eye then returned to his desk.

Toscana wore a short sleeved, white button down shirt with a red tie, loose around his neck. Did they even make shirts that could button up around that throat? His shoes must have cost five-hundred dollars. His skin was the color of sour skim milk. Salvator always thought it odd that a man like Toscana considered himself a doctor. He looked unhealthy. Salvator detested men like Toscana who lived their lives profiteering off the vanity of other people.

Rose Cavriaghi hugged her son. She was wearing a thin flower-printed sun dress, similar in cut to Anna's. In that dress, standing so close to Anna, Rose's thickness was striking. She could eat two platefuls of pasta and a few meatballs in one sitting, and still have room for a scoop or two of ice cream. Rose pushed Salvator back to get a better look at him, then smiled, leaned forward, and whispered: "You're so in love you cut your hand, eh?" She smiled at him again. Flicked up her eyebrows once or twice.

Salvator smiled back. Nodded. Rolled his eyes a little. He kissed Rose on the cheek. At one point, maybe six or seven years ago, her eyes had had that quality of warm, yellow sunshine that makes even the hardest rock soft. Now, though, her eyes had lost their warmth. During these last few years, what had for so long been a warm and patient quality in her eyes had devolved into the terminally disgusted look people in a hurry get when they're trying to speed and everyone else is going the speed limit. Salvator attributed this to the significant decrease in Capital 'R' Romance in her life. Though both she and Claudio were in their sixties, Claudio's sixty-four looked more and more like seventy-four and her sixty-two looked more and more like forty-three. Not even the meditation she'd been practicing had brought her out of her funk. Rose stared at him for a moment. And he couldn't read her. Her thick arms, her plump legs, her short, dark hair, straight like vermicelli. He thought: I love you, Mom; but all he said was, "How'd you get here so fast?"

Rose rubbed Salvator's back with her right hand. "Not that fast. You were in there forty minutes."

Salvator looked at Anna who was deep in conversation with her father. Toscana had her right bicep gripped in his fist. Anna tried to yank free.

"Really?" Salvator said, responding to his mother, but looking past her to Anna. That son of a bitch, he thought.

"Good thing Anna stopped by," Rose said.

"Mom," he said, finally looking at her, "I would endure a thousand more stitches to have her come by the shop again." Toscana's grip on Anna's arm tightened. "Hey," Salvator said, taking a step towards Anna and Toscana, "you don't need to hold her like that."

"What did you say?" Toscana said. He turned to face Salvator, though he did not release his grip on Anna's arm. He dragged her forward a step.

Claudio rubbed his forehead and swore. He pinched the bridge of his nose with the thumb and forefinger of his right hand. "You better forget about her, Salvator, and get over here." Claudio looked at Toscana with what Salvator perceived as apology. "She's seventeen and you're twenty-three. You go to jail just for thinking the thoughts you're thinking."

Salvator turned and said to Claudio: "You have no idea what I'm thinking," then he turned back to face Arturo Toscana. "I don't like you," Salvator said to the man. Salvator shook his head and, still looking at Toscana, said to Anna, "It's okay, Anna. You're going to be okay."

Arturo Toscana thrust a finger within inches of Salvator's face. Wish I knew some of that ninjutsu stuff Paulo knows, Salvator thought, because I'd really like to snap that thing off and ram it up his nose. "You don't talk to my daughter," Arturo Toscana said. "You ruined my car."

"Rose," Claudio said, loud enough for Salvator to hear, "our son here is acting like a stupid little boy. He's too old for her, and they're too rich for us." He nodded towards Toscana, who clearly agreed.

Salvator turned to face his parents. "Why don't you take a second and stand up for me here, Dad? Huh? Why don't you tell this guy he isn't welcome in our store anymore? Huh? Why don't you tell him you don't like the way he treats your son?"

Claudio said nothing.

The pitch between Arturo and Anna then crescendoed, and, when Salvator looked over, he saw Arturo's puffy white hand grab Anna's left arm. He grabbed and shook her hard enough that she nearly fell over this time. Tears streamed down her face. "I'm sorry," she was saying, over and over again. "You asked me to go get it!" she said. "I was just trying to help him."

At that moment, Salvator thought seriously about killing Arturo Toscana.

Toscana and Anna turned to leave, and Anna did not turn around to say good-bye.

Salvator pushed past his parents and walked right up to Anna's side and said, in as tender a voice as he could muster: "I have seen the shining star of morning." He lightly ran his hand down her bare arm.

She turned and half-smiled, tears still streaming from her eyes.

Arturo Toscana turned and shouted, "Back off!" He let go of Anna's arm and violently pushed Salvator away.

Other people in the waiting room had become agitated, visibly disturbed by the raised voices.

Now Salvator bent down on one knee, put his left hand to his heart, and stretched his right hand out in front of him, palm up. He closed his eyes and began to sing to her in an Italian operatic accent:

> *Tutti gli angeli*
> *portano la tua faccia,*
> *amore mio*

> All angels
> wear your face,
> my love

Arturo and Anna sped up in the direction of the door.

> *La tua presenza supera lo splendore del cielo,*
> *ferma le stagioni*

> Your presence outshines the heavens,
> stills the seasons

Anna turned and smiled, still crying; Salvator's voice rose in pitch:

> *Loro sono indegne*
> *fino che sorridi*

> They are unworthy
> until you smile

The Toscana's were out the door now.

†

Damon started back over to Claudio, but Claudio waved him off and said, "I'm sorry for this, Damon. We are leaving right now."

Claudio Cavriaghi went to grab Salvator, but Salvator pushed him away and stepped into the parking lot behind Toscana and Anna.

Rose yanked at Claudio's arm and held him back: "Leave him alone," she said.

"Leave him alone?" Claudio said, his eyes bulging. "He's causing a scene! He's making us look like a bunch of crazies!" He tried to pull away, but she held him tight. He sucked in and bit down on his lips, then, his finger an inch from Rose's nose: "You and your goddamn Caruso!"

Anna ducked into her father's other car—a spanking new Cadillac parked in the handicap zone. "Drive it home," Toscana shouted, spit hurling from his mouth, soggy words splattering on the driver's side window.

Salvator raised his voice till it cracked, hoping she'd hear him

> *Tutte delle mie speranze sono te;*
> *la ricompensa che ofre l'amore;*
> *il tuo bel nome mormorato*

> All my hopes are you;
> the reward love offers;
> your fair name whispered

Toscana stuttered something about "ruined car"—Salvator didn't quite catch what—turned, and got into his blood-stained Chevrolet parked three spaces away.

Salvator turned to his father and smiled. "You," he said, pointing at Claudio, "will not be able to keep me away from her." Then he wiggled his thumb over his shoulder. "And neither will he."

"That's what you think, huh?" Claudio said. "You think you talk to me like that, it's okay?" They were all in the parking lot now. Claudio took

†

Rose by the arm and said to her, loud enough so Salvator could hear: "He will not see that girl while he lives in my house."

The sun was low on the horizon, but its heat lingered, a too-heavy blanket on an already too-hot day. Salvator followed behind his parents. "Goddamn heat," Claudio said, and spit.

"It's supposed to get hotter," Rose said.

Salvator looked at her, stuck out his lower lip, and nodded. He kicked a rock into the street. He wanted to carve the heart out of Arturo Toscana and serve it to his father, prove to both of them he was no stupid little boy.

Four

Salvator Cavriaghi woke the next morning feeling more rested than he'd expected. The hand had throbbed half the night, but once the painkillers kicked in—he hadn't taken them till he couldn't stand it anymore—he slept well. He'd dreamed he was in a vast field and just in front of him was a huge bull goring a small calf. In the dream, he just stood there, naked, watching.

His bedroom was only large enough to fit his twin bed, the antique four-drawer dresser he'd gotten from his Uncle Svevo for his thirteenth birthday, and a small desk he, Salvator, had constructed out of scrap wood he'd found behind Cavriaghi's Meats. He'd spent many nights in this room as a child, sleeping with the light on some years, then trying to make the room as dark as possible in other years. Around the age of fourteen, he'd asked his parents if he could paint the room black and board up his windows with plywood. This did not happen. Save for a few framed photographs of Salvator and his family, the walls of the room were blank. He'd gone to St. Augustine's high-school in Oakland after graduating from the eighth grade at St. Peter's, but during high school he kept to himself, not out of choice, but more out of necessity. He worked over forty hours a week while in high school, and during the hours he wasn't working, he was

✝

either studying or practicing cutting meat, and doing the latter most often at his father's urging.

Salvator sat up and swung his legs over the side of the bed. He was only wearing boxers. Already he could see the faint creases in his torso that would, in another decade, become genuine wrinkles. He rubbed his belly with his right hand, then said out loud, "I promise you, one of these days you will be strong." His belly had heard that before. Three steps from the side of the bed was the dresser. He knew, even with the lights off—which they weren't—that his belt and wallet were exactly at chest level on the top right edge of the dresser. He knew if he opened the second drawer from the top and reached in to the back left side he'd find a clean pair of under-wear. But it wasn't dark; the sun was out and stretching its heat and yellow light through lazy gray clouds and into Salvator's room.

He dressed in an old pair of blue jeans and a plain green T-shirt, went into the kitchen to get some orange juice, and found the note on the table:

> *Didn't want to wake you. Went to yoga, then going*
> *shopping. Be back around noon.*   *Mom*

Salvator nodded and stuck out his lower lip. It was already 8:00 a.m. The pain-killers must have really knocked him out. How could he not have heard her leave? Surely his body's clock had accustomed itself to get-ting up at 3:30 a.m. by now. He poured the orange juice and sat down at the table. A memory from the previous day slipped from his subconscious mind into consciousness: Arturo Toscana's hand wrapped around Anna's left arm. He wondered how she was doing, and he wondered why, of all yesterday's events, that's the one his mind offered him.

He sipped the orange juice and its tartness made him pucker. Last night, after they'd returned from the hospital, Salvator called Nino and told him what had happened.

"Jesus," Nino had said. "She comes walking in the shop and I knew it as soon as I seen it, like she just reached right over Claude's shoulder—boy

---
✝
---

was he steamin'!—and into your chest, took your heart out, put it in her purse, and left."

"You think my dad's pissed?"

"He was pissed before that quarter you dropped yesterday hit the floor."

It surprised Salvator that Nino hadn't taken the opportunity to thoroughly harass him. Later though, after thinking about it some, Salvator figured Nino, himself an artist with meat, spared Salvator the razzing because Nino knew Salvator felt bad enough, or, probably more likely, Nino figured Paulo would harangue Salvator hard enough for everybody on the avenue.

Salvator took another sip of the orange juice, looked at his bandaged hand—which didn't hurt anywhere near as bad as he thought it would—and went out the front door of the house. Already, at a few minutes after eight in the morning, the heat felt like a lava bath. He couldn't believe he'd slept so late. Was Anna up? He must have fallen asleep around the time he usually got up. Salvator breathed in deeply through his nose, filling his lungs with the hot, clean air. How long had it been since he'd been home at this hour on a weekday? Five, six years? At least. He walked to the edge of the walkway. To his left, the garage Claudio had converted from a carport fifteen years earlier. To his right, the exterior wall of his parents' room.

Built in the 40's, the light-green, single story home, with its flat, black tar roof and neatly trimmed ivy hedge that ran along the sidewalk was the home Claudio and Rose bought when they first married. Salvator had been born there; well, actually, he was born in Providence hospital in Oakland, but this was the only home he'd ever lived in, and he was, in fact, conceived within its walls. He often wondered if his parents, in a particularly horny moment some twenty odd years into their marriage, had taken each other on the floor of the kitchen with a pot of meatballs boiling over on the stove. The front of the house looked small, though that was deceiving because inside Claudio and Rose had turned what was a three bedroom, one bath house when they bought it into a four bedroom house with two baths and an exterior workroom connected to the back of the house. Outside, at the front of the house, to Salvator's left, was the driveway, which sloped steeply up into the garage. To the left of the garage, where Salvator now stood, was a narrow walkway that led up to the front door of the house. Next to the front door was a window that opened onto the dining room, and along the walls of the walkway leading up to the door, a window into the garage and on the other side a window opening out from the master bedroom. The master bedroom had two very large windows that faced the street. A small lawn edged with juniper bushes and ivy fronted the house. The front yard was small, though: not even big enough for a swing set.

Salvator studied the roadway across the street from the house. Highway 13. It was raised above his street. One of his earliest memories was the construction of the highway. He remembered his father telling him once that that side of the street was, at one point, nothing but dirt. The state decided to put in a "connecting" freeway to connect the big highway 580 that ran north and south along Oakland's east edge, to the Caldicott tunnels, which, if highway 13 hadn't been put in could take as long as forty-five minutes. With 13 in, that trip was cut down to about fifteen minutes.

Salvator turned and went back inside. To the right of the front door was the dining room and to the left was the master bedroom. Beyond the dining room was the kitchen, where they spent most of their time. Maybe his father would let him invite Anna over for dinner.

The kitchen, though small, was useful. Rose prepared most of the food on the solid, foot-and-a-half thick, old-fashioned butcher's block in the middle of the kitchen. Just beyond the block a couch faced a television and behind the couch, which jutted out from the far wall, a table just big enough for four people, four plates, four cups, and a bowl of food in the center. During the holidays, when many people would show up—cousins, aunts, uncles—Claudio and Rose would have dinner in the dining room, where they could stretch out their fancy table and seat as many as fifteen adults.

†

The temperature outside was eighty degrees, which made the temperature inside at least ninety. Even with fans blowing in the front and back doors, circulating the air, it remained hot. One eighty foot tall redwood towering over the back yard provided little shade in the afternoon because the sun had already made its way around the tree. And the house's flat, black tar roof…well, it was all Salvator could do to stay cool. It seemed as if God was pissed off. The heat had gotten so bad that the only possible explanation was that somewhere on the planet, somebody had screwed up really bad, and God, it just so happened, was taking it out on Oakland. People were actually dying from the heat, plopping down right in the street, dead.

Rose kept the inside of the house immaculate. She would get very angry if anybody, especially Salvator, who "should know better," came in with dirty shoes. Oh, and don't ever sit on those love seats! Those are for guests! And even when guests are here I don't get to sit in them, Salvator thought. He would now, with the two weeks off from work, sneak a seat in the love seats.

The dining room was not extravagant—the two love seats, the piano in one corner, his mother's china cabinet, the polished table, the unused fireplace on the west wall—but Rose, like any self-respecting Sicilian woman, needed a place to serve guests, a place separated from the place she served her family. "Mom," Salvator had asked once, at the Christmas table, with a couple of friends and relatives present—Claudio had covered his eyes, apparently sensing that Salvator was about to do something wrong—"why do Mr. and Mrs. Foscolo get to eat at this table every time they come over, but I only get to eat here when they come over? Are they more specialer than me?"

As Salvator walked around the house, he began to sense how clean the place really was, something he just now realized he'd been taking for granted for far too long. He ran his finger over the top edge of the bathroom door moulding. No dust. He shook his head and smiled. Amazing, he thought. It's no wonder she never sits down. Every night, the table is set, the food is hot—and there was always a lot of food. He thought: my mother doesn't have a life. She lives her life keeping my life clean.

He sat down in the kitchen, at the table, and began to think. Yes, the sounds of home. Though the house was now completely silent, he could hear everything. The television droning in the background. The crackling of something frying on the stove, or the scrape of a spoon as Rose stirred some pasta. He could hear his father snoring in the recliner, his father yelling from the garage. He could hear the washing machine going in the back of the house, the dryer knocking around a pair of shoes, making a racket. He got up and walked back to the laundry room. The door to the room wasn't closed, but a curtain hung in the doorway. He looked in. Washer. Dryer. His mother's sewing machine. Shelves of sewing books, cook books, and a rack of encyclopedias—he hadn't seen the encyclopedias in years, he'd thought she'd gotten rid of them. She kept the room neat. There was a garbage bag near the dryer, full of lint, and beside that a laundry basket full of what looked from Salvator's perspective to be rags. The laundry detergent and bleach were neatly placed on a shelf above the machines. A piece of dark green material sat crumpled on the edge of the sewing machine, and next to the material was a pattern book, pages down. Salvator picked up the pattern book. She was making a blouse for someone.

I work all day, Salvator thought, outside of the house, but look at the work she does here! She makes clothes! She keeps the tops of doors clean!

Salvator put the sewing book back down as he'd found it, then left the laundry room.

It was interesting. He'd been alone in the house now for an hour or so and save for a few pictures on the walls, his father felt absent. Everything he'd thought was about his mother because all he could see around him was his mother: the sewing machine in there, the other clean rooms, her magazine on the couch. His father had left no impression on the house. He remembered when he was six or seven or eight years old, rushing to the front window of the house, the night air cool, his father on his way home

from work. Salvator would sniff the air, convinced he could smell his
father coming home, certain he could smell the meat miles before it got
home. But now, standing in the kitchen, he couldn't smell his father. He
couldn't see his father. Was it because his mother so meticulously picked
up after him? After everybody. Even Claudio's newspaper was gone. Was
this his father's fault? His mother's?

Salvator opened the refrigerator. There he found signs of his father:
wrapped steaks, a stick of salami, some tripe, a gallon of his favorite
lemonade. Salvator took out the salami and the lemonade, poured some
lemonade in over the orange juice in his glass, and cut off the heel of the
salami and ate it.

He walked to the guest room. Another spotless room. His parents had
always said that a guest should have a nice clean room. Salvator picked up
the lamp on the desk. It was a small lamp, one his mother had given him
when he was three years old. Her father had given it to her. The lamp had
a glass shade over the top of it shaped like an upside down rose. It was
made in Sicily back in the late 1800's, his mother had told him, by her
Great Uncle Saverio on her father's side. Uncle Saverio, his mother had
said, was the greatest glass blower of the family, perhaps the greatest in
Sicily. His mother had a large family: three sisters and six brothers. One of
her sisters, the oldest, Serenella, was a school teacher who'd died of cancer
twenty-two years earlier while Rose was pregnant. Her other two sisters,
Carlotta and Angelica, were born so close together (hardly a year between
them), and looked so much alike, everyone called them the twins. Five
years after Rose and Salvator married, Carlotta married Danilo, a working
jazz bassist she'd met in a San Francisco restaurant. To the dismay of both
of the families, Danilo and Carlotta chose not to have children. "Are they
even Sicilian?" someone asked. "Maybe they're on drugs," another said.
They wanted to travel around with Danilo's band, Trio, without the bur-
den of having to worry about schools and friends. Rose and Claudio
thought that perhaps once Carlotta got the idea in her head that maybe
she'd like to have a job of her own, she and Danilo would settle down in

their San Francisco apartment and start having kids. This, though, Carlotta thwarted by taking up photography and writing and selling pictures and articles to magazines all over the country on the towns she and Danilo visited. A job she could do anywhere. Rose's other sister, Angelica, never married. She left California to go to college in New York City. She wanted to be an actress, "Like Claudia Cardinale," she would say. Angelica never came back. In fact, she never even answered any of Rose's letters. Salvator remembered his father and mother talking about it.

"Do you think she's ashamed?" Rose asked.

"What does she have to be ashamed of?" Claudio asked.

"I don't know," Rose said, shaking her head and lifting her eyebrows. "I don't know."

Rose's brothers? Two of them died in wars. Marco in Korea and John in Viet Nam. Rose never knew Marco and barely remembered John. She was twelve when John died, but he'd been all over the world in the Army and she'd only seen him a few times. Her other brothers? Well, Svevo, the oldest of her siblings, still laid bricks in Pittsburgh, forty-minutes behind them on the other side of the Oakland Hills. They saw him rarely because Svevo did not like anybody. Not men, not women. "A bunch of hypocrites, the lot of you," he would say. The only two people that Svevo could commiserate with—though he had never met them—were George Carlin and Lenny Bruce. But for every ounce of anger and hate he spewed into the world, he put an equal ounce of love and compassion into his bricks. He was the last of his kind in Pittsburgh. In fact, just a few years ago, a young student from the university in Berkeley who said he was working on a Ph.D.—"Piled high and deep," Svevo liked to say—had contacted Salvator because he, the student, had heard that Salvator's father knew a brick-layer in Pittsburgh and was wondering if Claudio could put him in contact with the brick-layer. "I'm writing my dissertation on Sicilian artisans," the man had said to Claudio. What Salvator didn't know at the time was that his evil and vile and hate filled uncle—whom Salvator adored—was only one of four old-school Sicilian brick-layers in the country. The other three lived in Chicago,

†

Jersey City, and Fort Lauderdale, respectively. It turned out that the student's work and study of Svevo's work was one of the first modern attempts to catalog the methods of the ancient art. What struck Salvator most was how the student talked about Svevo's "generosity" and "kindness." Had the man found the right Svevo?

Rose's other brothers, Horace, Frank, and Joseph, the youngest three of her siblings, were spread out across the country. Horace, last they'd heard, was a welder in Michigan; Frank was a drummer in a rock band; and Joseph lived with his three dogs a few miles south of Oakland, in Hayward.

As for Claudio, he was an only child who came late, and as a surprise, to his mother and father. His mother had suffered six miscarriages over the course of ten years. At the time, Claudio's parents decided to take in foster kids so that they'd at least have some children around the house. Then, Claudio's mother, at thirty-eight, got pregnant again. His parents were scared, happy, and apprehensive. His father was ten years older than his mother. But when after three months the doctor said, "You're going to have this one," they celebrated. Claudio sprang from his mother's path, a healthy nine pound, ten ounce Sicilian boy.

Claudio had grown up for the first nine years of his life with foster children coming in and out of the house. Then, suddenly, his parents decided to stop taking in foster kids, and Claudio grew up on his own. But he did not regret this. He had many close friends at school, and his parents were always lenient when it came to things like sleep-overs and, eventually, dating. They'd told him once, when he was twenty, right after he'd married Rose, that they didn't want him to feel lonely, without friends.

What Salvator remembered most about his own childhood, from as far back as his memory would go, were the times he spent learning the art of cutting meat with his father.

He remembered one time, his father standing over him, teaching him how to sharpen a knife. "Here, Salvator," Claudio had said, "like this." And his father took the knife and pulled it smoothly along the whet stone. The day was cool, and fog hung over the hills in beautiful frothy wisps.

"Life is like the edge of a blade, Salvator," Claudio said. "It can be long, or it can be short. It can be dull, or it can be sharp." He ran his thumb across the edge of the knife. "It can cut you if you do not pay attention, and you must treat it, as you must treat everything, with dignity and respect." Salvator, a seven-year-old then, listened intently, worshipped at his father's block. "You must work hard, Salvator, and provide for your family. I don't care what you do, as long as its honorable and doesn't hurt anyone. If you choose to cut meat, you will not get rich, but you will also not go hungry."

He went to his parents' bedroom, which was large, big enough for their queen size bed, a dresser each for his mom and dad, and a small antique desk at which Rose did their bills. Salvator walked over to Rose's dresser and, with his right hand, pocketed the four quarters beside the jewelry box, while with his left hand he picked up the small framed photograph of his parents on their wedding day. He sat down on their bed and looked at the picture. It was in black and white. Claudio and Rose had had a choice between color and black and white pictures and opted for the black and white ones because both their parents' had had their wedding photos done in black and white. Rose was wearing a white, lacey dress that went to her ankles. And she was smiling, her head tilted back and her chin up, holding her bouquet. Claudio was wearing a black tuxedo with a black bow-tie. Behind them, the church's altar, adorned in white carnations. Claudio had his left arm around Rose's back. Their free hands hung at their sides. In this photo, Claudio's eyes were closed and Rose was smiling broadly, laughing. The photographer had asked them to pose, and Claudio, always one to take any opportunity to make Rose laugh—at least back then it was true—said he'd need a moment to prepare. He closed his eyes, wiggled his fingers as if he were trying to remember some important fact, and said, "I must meditate for a moment," then proceeded to keep his face perfectly still. Rose laughed then, knowing the photographer thought Claudio was serious, and, in the instant the photographer realized he was having his leg pulled, he snapped the picture. And charged them for it. But it was their favorite photo. Ten minutes after that photograph was taken, the formal they keep framed in the living room was taken, both of them posing, fake smiling, photo smiling. Rose, Salvator knew, loved most this photo in his hands. It showed his parents being themselves; it showed them as genuine people, being silly; it showed them *being* the reason they married each other.

Salvator put the photograph back where he found it, then looked at himself in his father's mirror. He held his bandaged hand up and turned it around a few times. No blood had seeped through the bandage. The wound of the heart in his hand. There it was; love's deep cut. The doctor had done a good job with the stitches. He looked at his hair, at the black crescent moons under his eyes. Bags, his father'd called them. Ugly bags from too much work and I'm not even old yet. Surely Anna would not love such darkly circled eyes. Salvator shook his head and leaned forward. He stared at his own eyes in the mirror. Don't look away, he told himself. Look! Look at yourself. Those brown, bloodshot eyes. What's in there Salvator? What do you have to show for yourself besides a wound? Salvator's mind wanted to look away, but his heart had other plans, now that it had finally gotten him to the mirror. Oh yes, Salvator, look closely, because that's you, that's you back in there behind the iris, young and strong and in love with a seventeen year old. Love? Seventeen? What am I thinking? he thought. His mind tried harder to move away from the mirror, and, for a second, he thought it had won because he started to turn away, but then his heart focused the brunt of its strength in one deadly question: Why are you afraid to look, Salvator?

He shook his head again. What the hell was he doing talking to himself in the mirror? Was he some kind of nut?

He left the bedroom and returned to the kitchen. He took a piece of round steak from the refrigerator and threw it on the block, pulled a carving knife from the drawer to the right of sink, then, frustrated, suddenly realizing he only had one hand to work with, Salvator Cavriaghi stabbed the knife through the steak and into the block. "Goddamn it," he said aloud, instantly sorry he'd used that particular phrase to express his anger.

And it was anger that welled up in him. And why the hell shouldn't he say Goddamn it out loud if that's what he felt in his heart? It's not like God didn't know what he was thinking. And then he said it, out loud, waving his bandaged hand at the block: "Goddamn meat, goddamn knife, goddamn cut in my hand, goddamn stupid butcher. Goddamn mirror!" He slapped the block with his good hand. He was no more than a reflection of his parents. Working class. Hard working class. A never-late-for-work-never-take-a-day-off family. Even Rose, who never left the house to go to work got up with Claudio and Salvator to make them breakfast.

As Salvator stood over the block, looking at the steak impaled with his carving knife, he thought: "What are my chances? Her parents are a doctor and a lawyer. Our house barely costs as much as her parents' cars!"

He pulled the knife out of the steak, cleaned it, put it and the steak back, then went back to bed.

He'd already fallen asleep when Rose returned.

Five

"Look," Claudio was saying, through half a mouthful of peas, "it doesn't matter how much they offer, I'm not taking it."

"Jesus dad—" Salvator said.

"Salvator," Rose said, looking at him and touching his arm, "please don't use the Lord's name in vain."

Salvator pushed on. "But they're offering you half a million dollars." He flipped both of his hands up, dropping his napkin: "Half a *million* dollars," he said again. "That's twice as much as the building is worth, and probably four times as much as you've got saved for retirement."

"How do you know how much I've got saved for retirement?" Claudio said. He waved his hand at Salvator in one quick motion, as if he were trying to flick away a fly, "You don't know anything."

Claudio had brought home the news: Richard Head, of the Hunter, Head, Markum, and Slaughter law firm—"the same one that Anna's mother works at"—had come in to the shop and told Claudio that his firm had been hired to represent Ultra Mart, a six year old chain store based in Cupertino "that in the last three years has increased its number of stores from ten to twenty-three by buying up land in urban areas no one else will buy. They've come to the city and offered to put an Ultra Mart in across the street, which would provide hundreds of new jobs in the area, if they could also buy this side of the street to put in a restaurant and parking lot."

Claudio chewed through a bite of the breaded meat. "They not only want to take the businesses down," he said, "but all the houses behind us, too!" He wiped his mouth with his napkin. "I just can't believe it. The whole damn block."

Here they were, facing another head on confrontation with that ineluctable steel wrecking ball the "authorities" called progress.

Claudio shook his head.

Rose spoke: "Salvator, if your father doesn't want to sell, don't fight him."

"I'm not trying to fight," Salvator said. "I'm just thinking, Dad. You were going to retire in another year anyway. Why not retire now with a lot more money?"

"Salvator, you know damn well and good this has nothing to do with money and everything to do with my sense of duty. They take my store down and I'm fucking dead."

Rose immediately stood and took her plate to the sink.

"I love my store," Claudio said. "I'm a *butcher*," he said. He held his hands over the table and extended them to Salvator. "See that," he said, pointing with his right forefinger at the mangled tip of his left forefinger. "That's why I'm a butcher." He paused and rested his arms on the table, two thick and twisted roots. "Eighteen years old when I did it, and my father was standing two feet away. He laughed and laughed when he saw the tip of my finger on my block. He never grabbed my hand, Salvator, he grabbed the chunk I'd cut off my finger, rubbed it between his thumb and fingers and said, 'Now you are a butcher,' then he threw my finger tip in the trash can and went on cutting his meat. 'Now you are a butcher.' He said it twice. And it wasn't until that day that I realized"—Claudio slowed down, staring at his hands—"I was a butcher because I had to be a butcher. I give up my store, and I give up my father, and my uncles, and my grand-father, and every other goddamn Cavriaghi that came before me."

Salvator moved to speak, but Claudio stopped him.

"I never thought you'd want me to sell the store, Salvator. The way you cut meat…don't you want to cut meat, Salvator?"

"Of course I do," Salvator said.

"Then what do you mean 'think about selling the store'?"

"I never thought about it like you just said. It's just you were talking about all that money, I figured you and Mom, you guys could retire."

"What's 'retire?'" Claudio said. "What's that mean? You've been tired before, then stopped being tired for awhile, now you get to be tired again? Who the hell wants that?" Rose came over and took their plates away. Claudio leaned forward in his chair. "When you get to be my age, Salvator, there isn't a whole hell of a lot more you want to do than what you already know how to do. We retire and what, you think your mother's going to stop cleaning the house? You think she's going to stop playing her piano? You think I'm going to stop cutting meat? All of a sudden, just like that?" He snapped his fingers.

"You take that money and Mom could hire somebody to clean the house."

"There isn't a team of twenty people could keep this house as clean as your mother. And besides, even if there was, she'd drive them all crazy telling them they aren't doing a good enough job!"

Salvator suspected his father was right on this count.

"I take that money, Salvator, and I'm living on dirty money, I'm feeding my family and paying my bills with shit money, you understand? There's no way in hell I'm selling my store. They want it, they're going to have to come in and take it. I don't care how much money they wave at me."

"Can we talk about something else now?" Rose said from the sink, where she was washing dishes. "Don't you think that little Anna's a cute girl, Claudio?

Salvator winced.

"Oh she's cute," he said. "But you can forget about this one here going out with her."

"Says who?" Salvator said.

"Says your father," Claudio said.

Rose turned around, her hands dripping soap suds, "I don't think it's so bad, Claudio, really. He obviously likes the girl."

"He dropped a hindquarter of meat and sliced his hand wide open because of her," Claudio said. "He even thinks about her and he won't be able to cut meat."

"You didn't know Mom the first time you saw her, either, and you told me you fell in love with her the instant you saw her." Salvator folded his arms.

"She's too young, too rich, and her mother works for the people trying to tear down my shop." Claudio looked away for a moment.

"You're six years older than Mom, and her parents are something like twelve or fifteen years apart. And who cares how much money they have? I don't."

"You're not going out with her, and that's it. Don't bring it up again," Claudio said.

Rose dried her hands and spoke directly to Claudio: "I understand you don't like her parents, Claudio, but that's not the girl's fault."

"I don't care," Claudio said. "I don't want anything to do with her."

"Nobody's asking you to have anything to do with her," Salvator said. "You think I gotta do what you say?" He regretted that one.

Claudio stared at Salvator. Claudio nodded. Claudio said: "You think you're going to talk to me like that and I'm going to be nice to you? You don't know anything."

Rose moved towards the table. Claudio held up his hand, stopping her.

"You know what Salvator," Claudio said. "You do whatever the hell you want, just do it away from me. Huh?"

Salvator got up from the table, said, "For a minute there when you were talking about your dad and your finger, I thought you were human." He wanted to jam a fork into his father's hand. "But now that I think about it, it was probably really only about fifteen seconds that I thought that."

Claudio clenched his fists and grit his teeth. "Rose," he said, then waved it off, disgusted. "Get out," Claudio said, looking at the center of the table. "Take you and all your talk and get out."

SIX

Salvator knocked once, entered Nino's apartment, threw his keys on the long kitchen counter, and called for Nino, who came out from the bathroom with shaving cream on his face and a towel wrapped around his nether regions.

"Hey kid," Nino had said. "What're you doing here?"

"You got some time to talk?" Salvator said. He could see into Nino's bedroom—the unmade bed, the clothes bunched-up in the basket, the polished pine of the night stand. Five weeks after Nino's wife left him, Tom Polaski offered Nino this apartment above the hardware store. Polaski's tenant was moving away for another job, and, knowing Nino's situation, Polaski wanted to give Nino "first crack at filling it up."

"Yeah, I got plenty of time," Nino said. He pointed at the couch. "Sit down. I'll be done in a minute."

Just beyond the edge of the kitchen countertop was a sliding bay window that opened out onto a small, private deck. Salvator slid the door open then put his hands on his lower back and bent backwards, stretching his chest and stomach muscles. It was still hot out. He fixed himself a peanut-butter and jelly sandwich, filled a glass with water, then sat down in Nino's living room to eat and watch Jeopardy. While scientists studying the cosmos or quantum theory may need to measure time in nanoseconds, persons entering the House of Di Lampedusa must measure time in ninoseconds, which correspond proportionally either to the amount of food left on Nino's plate or the amount of clothing he needs to put on. When Nino is at the towel stage of dressing himself, as now, a ninosecond could stretch time out as long as twenty or thirty regular seconds.

Salvator took a bite of his sandwich and, his mind peripherally connected to the television, he began to wander into the realm of self-deprecation, as he always did when he got into it with his father. He imagined himself as the only contestant on Beelzebub's Twisted Jeopardy:

"I'll take 'Royal Pains In The Ass' for thirty-two cents, Satan."

The Vile and Venomous One read from the Helleprompter: "He's the old Sicilian butcher who played the wicked, love-thwarting, soul-dashing scrooge in Frank Capra's brilliant documentary, *It's a Pitiful Life*."

"Who is my father?"

"That's correct," The Prince of Pain says. "Select again."

The audience—a raucous collection of demi-urges, minor demons, decrepit renegades, and major villains—boo's and hisses. "Filet him, Asmodeus!" one of them shouts. The Devil points a crooked, decaying claw at the minuscule fiend and turns him into steaming cow dung.

Salvator: "I'll take 'Chumps' for a buck-and-a-quarter you hellhound bastard."

The Devil smiles at the compliment, flutters his fecal eyelashes. He coughs up some blood, a sign, according to some of his imps, that the Infinitely Malignant One actually likes you and would consider sparing your limp soul from eternal damnation if you continued to shower him with septic effluent.

The Devil read the next answer: "This gaunt-faced, pencil-necked, stinky-shit-leaving, father-ignoring ignoramus whose fallen in love with a beautiful little piece of cake I personally wouldn't mind snacking on wants to know what he should do now."

"Me," Salvator says.

"Oh, no," the Foul Fiend says. "I'm sorry." He grimaces, then bites off the tip of one of his toes, chews it for a moment, then spits it out. "You have to phrase your answer in the form of a question. I'm afraid we'll have to remove one of your testicles."

The devil calls to his other form, offstage: "Lucifer? The rusty butter knife please."

Now the audience roars with laughter.

"Don't bother," Salvator says, holding up his hand and laughing with the congregation of shadows. "They apparently took those when they circumcised me."

Nino shouted from the bathroom, snapping Salvator from his reverie: "Whyn't you fix yourself a sandwich or something? I'll be out in a minute."

Salvator rolled his eyes and put his sandwich down when he caught a whiff of Nino's cologne. "Jesus Christ, Nino," Salvator said, "are you bathing in that crap?"

Nino didn't answer. Salvator remembered the day Nino's divorce papers came through. He went with Nino to the courthouse. Esme wore a tight business suit that day. It was the first time Nino had seen her in over nine weeks. "She's lost weight," Nino said to Salvator when she entered the room. Her face was smug, tight around the edges, and very red and shiny. Salvator thought she looked burned and Nino commented on her drooping lower right eyelid, barely exposing its pink, fleshy underside. It had never looked like that before. She wore a thin silk scarf around her neck. "I think she's finally had that face lift," Nino had whispered, though more to himself than to Salvator.

Nino came out of the bathroom twenty-five minutes later wearing pressed chinos and a fancy button-down denim shirt.

"You going somewhere?" Salvator asked.

"I got a date with Becky Shaw comes in the shop. Taking her to dinner."

"You said you got plenty of time." Not ten months ago, Claudio and Salvator had found Nino sprawled out on his butcher's block in the shop, a half-digested salami sandwich puked onto the floor beneath him.

Salvator had wiggled Nino's foot. "Get up." And within an hour Nino—nodding, defeated—had downed a pot of coffee, and agreed to call AA.

"I do," Nino said, pulling at his collar. "I don't have to meet her for another two hours." Nino sat down in the recliner across from Salvator. "So what's going on?"

"My dad says he won't go for me seeing Anna."

"That's it?" Nino said. "You're twenty-three years old. Grow up." He stood and went in to the kitchen.

"What the hell does that mean?"

"It means you sound like a baby, not like a man."

"He said he'd kick me out if I try to date her."

"You're twenty-three for Christ's sake! Don't wait for him to kick you out, *leave*." Nino took a glass from the cabinet and filled it with water. "I thought you came here to talk about something." He opened the refrigerator, looked in, then closed it. "You want to see her? See her. Don't whine about it."

"He'd kill you if he heard you say that."

"You're stupid. I've known your father for over thirty years. He knows me, he knows I treat you like I'd treat my own son if I had one, and he knows you'd come talk to me, and he knows I don't bullshit around."

"So you're not going to give me any advice?"

"You want advice? Here's advice: be a man." He opened the refrigerator again and pulled out a block of cheddar cheese and a loaf of bread. He held them up to Salvator. Salvator shook his head. "You may be some big shot butcher," Nino said, lopping off a chunk of cheese and wrapping it in a slice of bread, "but you live with your parents. You think that's going to impress a woman?" Nino snorted and shook his head, took a bite of the makeshift sandwich. His mouth half-full of food: "You really are stupid."

"I thought you were an alcoholic, not an assoholic."

"And you're a comedian."

"So," Salvator said, "what's going on with you and that Becky Shaw woman? You guys got a thing?"

"Jesus," Nino said. "We're going out for dinner, it ain't like we're getting married." Then Nino shrugged. For a second, Salvator thought Nino looked shy, bashful even. "We might have a thing," Nino said.

"What the hell does she see in you?" Salvator said. "You're just a grouchy old man."

Nino snorted. "I'm telling you, you're stupid. Ever since Esme dumped me, it's been like I'm not even the same guy I was with her. When me and her got married, I was a drunk and she was a nut. Well, I ain't a drunk no more, you know what I mean?"

"Once a drunk, always a drunk. That's what you told me."

"Right, right. Whatever. I'm saying I don't drink no more." Nino waved the sandwich in Salvator's direction. "I'm a different person." Nino paused, considering something. Salvator waited. Nino continued: "Well, I'm the same person"—Salvator watched Nino think—"just different is all. Anyway, there's a guy comes to one of the meetings I go to. Real nice guy. I got to know him. Never see him outside of the meetings, but we talk it up a bit before each meeting, check in with each other, shoot the bull. This guy, he's a real big deal. Famous writer. Money out to here. Had it all, as they say. Fact is, he found out the hard way, he didn't have shit. He'd surrounded himself with people who *did* have shit, like his wife and kids. And by having shit I mean they didn't drink."

"Who was he?" Salvator said. "Have I heard of him?"

"It's Alcoholics Anonymous, you dumb ass, not Alcoholics Tell All Your Friends About Who Else Comes To The Meetings." Nino rubbed his forehead. "This guy, he's a good guy, good man. Just a real fucking drinker. Used to be, anyway. Made me wonder if I was even a drunk after I heard his story. Anyway, he had too much money to drink all of *that* away, but, like he said, he didn't have too much in the brain department, so that was gone pretty quick." Nino waved a hand in the air, took another bite of food. "Make a long story short. Guy loses everything. The wife, the kids, the job, damn near goes bankrupt, but didn't, like I said. Like one of his cheesy damn books. Finally he says 'Fuck it,' gets himself into AA, starts doing the steps, and realizes that, sure enough, he *was* an asshole. Goddamn stroke of genius. Whole family had every right to leave him cold." Nino slapped his forehead, as if he'd just had a dramatic realization.

Salvator said, "Where are you going with this, Nino? We were talking about your new girl friend."

"I'm getting there," Nino said. "So this guy, he starts going to meetings everyday, in the beginning anyway. Sometimes two or three meetings a day. Really getting in to the program. He's been sober something like ten years now. Well, anyway, after a year or two of sobriety, he meets this woman at his church and they hit it off. Now this is what he tells me when I tell him I met Becky: 'Take it slow, Nino. Because if you're anything like me, and I know you are or else we wouldn't be standing here talking, you'll want this one to be nice.' By 'this' he meant whatever kind of relationship came out of me meeting Becky, and by 'nice' I took him to mean not fucked-up by liquor. Well, he's a big believer in romance now, 'courting a woman,' as he calls it. And I'll be damned if he isn't right on the money. He buys her flowers, sends her cards, tells her how beautiful she is, how lucky he is to know her, all that kind of stuff. And you know what? It'd make you sick how happy these two are. Make you want to vomit."

"Sounds to me like you want that kind of illness, Nino," Salvator said.

"You're damn right I do. So what I'm getting at is that I took some of his hints and secrets and applied them to what I got going on with Becky. There is no greater happiness, Salvator, than courting a woman. Than *earning* her love." Nino grunted. "You can take that to the bank and cash it."

Salvator rolled his eyes and stood up. "Is this your way of telling me I should go for it with Anna?" He went in to the kitchen, took the rest of Nino's sandwich out of his hand, ate it in one bite, then went and unlocked the front door.

As Salvator opened the front door to leave, Nino said, "It's just my way of saying don't come back till you have some hair on your balls."

SEVEN

S alvator took a sip of water and laid back down on his bed and laced his fingers behind his head. He stared at the spider dangling from the ceiling about three feet above him. The spider didn't move.

Salvator made a mental list of his options: one, stay with his parents and never see Anna; two, stay with his parents, see Anna, get kicked out; and three, make the first move and move out of his parents' house, and get to see Anna. Number three led him to think of another possibility because he knew Claudio would never let him keep working at Cavriaghi's Meats if he moved out of his house on the pretense of wanting to see the girl. So Salvator modified number three and came up with: four, make the first move, move out of the house and find my own job and apartment.

This last one was most frightening and, he had to be honest, most exciting. He'd never done anything alone, really. He'd always been under the supervision of his mother and father, and more often than not it was his father. It was Claudio who made Salvator start working full time when he was thirteen, Claudio who insisted that Salvator stay late every night and practice cutting meat and sharpening knives. Salvator wondered, momentarily: Is this how other children feel? Like the ones who get famous in some sport by the time they're fourteen because their parents wouldn't let them do anything else but the sport when they were growing

✝

up? Like many of those children who would become, if only momentarily, a part of recorded history, Salvator finally had come to love his art. He saw the rewards Claudio had seen long before. He saw how the hard work had, quite literally, paid off. Once, when Salvator was very young, not even a butcher yet, Claudio said: "Sal, you only have to do one thing in this life to get by, but you have to do it extremely well. Better than anybody. You do that, you cut meat that way, you cut it like nobody else ever cut it, and you'll never be poor or hungry."

He thought about what he'd do if he actually did move out. He didn't really have any friends, save for Nino and Paulo, and though Paulo was close to Salvator's age, they weren't exactly compatible friends: unlike Paulo, Salvator did not have a Master's degree in Dating and Carousing. Nor did Salvator want to pursue those arts. He did have an interest in pursuing Anna Toscana, and he did think the chances of her falling in love with him would increase if he had his own apartment. That had to look good to a woman. Had to.

Salvator stood up from his bed and went to his closet. He removed a wooden box from the shelf in the closet and emptied the box's contents—cash—on his bed. This was all the money he'd saved over the last ten years. He didn't have a checking account because he didn't trust himself to be able to keep track of one, so he always had his father cash his paycheck right in the store. He rarely spent any money, and if he did, he spent it on things like taking his mom out to dinner, or buying Nino bags of hard candy. The bulk of the money he spent, which amounted to about seventy or eighty dollars a month, he spent on used books. Books on knives and butchery, books of poems, novels, whatever, and these books he kept only a short period of time, long enough to read them and then sell them back or exchange them for something else. He'd only kept a few of the books on butchery.

He had enough money in the box to rent an apartment, pay a few months rent, and buy a small used car.

"Jeez," he said aloud. He wiped his forehead.

✝

He wasn't convinced he wanted a car. He'd gotten around all these years without one of his own already—he always borrowed his dad's truck—and, though he knew that option would dissolve if decided to move out, he was experienced enough with the Oakland mass transit system that he could get around quite easily. Then again, if he wanted to take Anna out on dates, he'd have to have his own car.

He decided it: I'm moving out and buying my own car. Sleeping was definitely out of the question now because he had to consider where he'd look for an apartment, where he'd get a job—Safeway? Mayfair?—what kind of car he'd buy, how, doing all of this, he'd have time to court Anna.

The alarm clock in his parents' room went off. Salvator waited until his father rose and took a shower and until his mother had started making breakfast before he left his room.

They were in the kitchen, quietly going about their morning ritual: she making breakfast, he finishing the previous day's newspaper. Normally Salvator would be part of the picture too, helping his mother with breakfast, usually in the form of eating the bacon or toast before it got to the table. He stood in the doorway of the kitchen in his T-shirt and boxers.

Rose saw Salvator first. "Why are you up so early?" she said. "You should sleep in."

"Haven't slept," Salvator said, kissing his mom on the cheek.

Claudio did not look up from his paper.

"Hi Dad," Salvator said.

Claudio looked at Salvator, half-smiled, and jerked his head in an awkward nod, but he did not say anything.

They all came to the table and started serving themselves in silence.

"I've been thinking," Salvator said. He paused to eat a piece of bacon. "I've been thinking I want to move out and get my own place."

"You don't know the first thing about taking care of a house," Rose said. "Why would you want to do that?"

"Because it's time. I'm doing it. I already made up my mind."

"He already made up his mind," Claudio said to Rose. His voice floated up and down, emphasizing every other syllable: "He already made up his mind."

"You're not moving out, Salvator," Rose said. "That's ridiculous. It's one thing to have a crush on this girl, it's something else all together to think you can just move out. Where do you come with this all of a sudden?"

Salvator's voice strained a little more than he'd hoped: "I'm moving out."

"Let him go, Rose," Claudio said. "We can turn his room into an office."

"Don't you even care that I want to move out?"

"No," Claudio said, sucking air up through his nose.

"Thanks."

"You're not moving out, Salvator," Rose repeated.

"Yes I am. You expect me to live here with you two forever? You want me living here when I'm forty? Fifty? God knows I don't want to be here that long."

"Why all of a sudden with the wanting to move out?" Claudio said, finally looking at Salvator.

"I talked to Nino last night—"

"Nino's an asshole," Claudio said. "I don't know why the hell I ever hired him."

"He's your best friend and you know it. He said you'd know I'd go talk to him and that you knew what he'd say."

"He's an idiot," Claudio said, mumbling and waving his hand. "Telling my son he should move out. Is he the one going to put you up while you find a place to live? Because you won't be sticking around here. And you can sure as hell forget about coming into my shop."

"You're both way out of line," Rose said. "None of this matters. You're not moving out, Salvator."

"Yes I am, Mom, and if he's not going to let me live here until I find my own place, then I'll be out of here before he gets home from work."

"Where are you going to go?" she said. "You don't even know how to fold your clothes let alone wash them."

"I'm not stupid," Salvator said.

"I'm starting to wonder," Rose said.

EIGHT

By four o'clock Salvator had all the belongings he planned to take with him packed and ready to go. Five boxes of stuff: four boxes of clothes and one box of books. He left everything else behind and planned to use some of his savings to buy the things he'd need, like a bed and bedding and some kitchenware and some towels. He'd called Paulo and asked if he could store his stuff and himself there until he found a place to live. "No more than a week," Salvator said.

He loaded his boxes up into the truck—Rose drove Claudio to work that morning—at least they did that much—and drove them to Paulo's. Paulo had hidden an extra key behind one of the bushes in the walkway leading up to his door. Salvator let himself in, put the boxes in the spare bedroom that Paulo used as storage, and drove the truck to the back lot of Cavriaghi's Meats, where his father kept it most of the time. He didn't go into the shop to say hello, he just walked around the block to the bus stop and caught the next bus that took him within a couple miles of Paulo's place, then walked from there.

Salvator was asleep in the middle of the living room floor, feet splayed out wide, one arm twisted awkwardly over his head, the other at his side, when Paulo got home.

"Get up," Paulo said, kicking Salvator's foot.

"Hey," Salvator said, groggy. "Thanks for letting me stay here."

"No problem, man. You need anything?" He walked towards the kitchen.

"No. I'm good."

"Your father's pissed off to high heaven, man."

"So what."

"Well, he didn't say nothing to me, but man, you should have seen him with the customers, yelling at them, throwing their meat on the counter."

"He'll get over it," Salvator said.

"Did you see this?" Paulo handed Salvator a copy of the *Oakland Tribune*'s Classified section. He'd circled a couple of adds. For all his manly attributes—his hairy chest, his strong biceps, his thin mustache—Paulo always treated the slender and geeky Salvator with kindness. Paulo's reputation as a partier followed him everywhere. Friends of his would come in to the shop every day of the week and try "to set something up for the weekend." Paulo pointed at the paper. "Look at that last one there, the one with two circles around it. Looks like a good place."

Salvator read the add to himself: "One bedroom apartment over garage. Montclair. $800/month. No pets. Unfurnished. Water and Garbage paid. Call Morris 362-4360."

Salvator bobbed his head up and down, "Montclair. That'd sure be nice."

"Think you can afford it?" Paulo asked.

"I can right now, but I need to find work."

"You'll find work," Paulo said. "You should give them a call."

Salvator called and Morris, the landlord, explained that the apartment had one bedroom, a small living room/kitchen, and a small bath. There were laundry facilities in the garage below the apartment. And that he, Morris, "don't like no noise. Don't want no noisy bastards."

Salvator cupped the mouth piece of the telephone with his hand. "Hey, Paulo," he said. Paulo came out of his bedroom. "Can I borrow your car for a little bit? The guy says I can come look at it right now."

Paulo shook his head. "No way. I'll drive you."

†

The road climbed steeply. They passed streets lined with maples and small, stucco houses. Many of these houses had been built in the middle of the century, a few of them were older. Some of the older ones had one car garages that seemed too small to hold any car built after 1930. They drove through the northeast corner of Oakland and passed the outer edge of Piedmont, one of the wealthiest sections of the city. Salvator's father's richest customers lived in Piedmont in houses most of Salvator's relatives would call hotels: swimming pools and tennis courts and gated entries, ten and fifteen and twenty room houses with more people "on staff" than in the family.

"Hey," Paulo said. "Mind if we take a little detour? I want to see if my buddy's home."

Salvator shrugged. The man had said he'd be there all night and that Salvator could come by any time before nine. It was six-forty-five.

Paulo made a couple more turns, found what he was looking for—a spiffed-up 1967 Chevrolet Camaro, black—and mentioned that they might stop by on their way back from seeing Salvator's apartment. They did not return to the main road the same way they had come, and as they made another left, Salvator saw it, sparkling under the lights of a large, three-door white stucco garage: Arturo Toscana's green and white 1955 Chevrolet Bel Air.

"Slow down," Salvator said, looking out the passenger side window and waving his left hand at Paulo. "That's Toscana's car." Toscana's garage seemed larger than Salvator's entire house. Next to the car rested a tarp-covered boat on a trailer.

Paulo brought the Corvette to a complete stop. "What's this?" He let the engine idle.

The cement driveway, lined with bricks on both sides, curved slightly, like a barely recognizable 's.' To the left of the driveway and garage, and set back from the street by at least 100 feet, stood the house, a monstrous tribute to arches and stucco and terra cotta roofing. The size of the house reminded Salvator of his church. Jeezamarooni, he thought. A brick walkway, lined with miniature lamps, led to the front double doors, which, from Salvator's angle, looked more like the doors to a state capitol building than the doors to a home. "Talk about cash," Salvator said, shaking his head. "You'd think this guy was a millionaire or something." Salvator could see lights on in nearly all of the windows. There, inside the home, the stamp of opulence: polished hardwood walls; the faint, yellowish glow of antique reading lamps, their shades drooping like sad flowers; patterned wall paper—though he couldn't make out the pattern; a brighter light in a room far to the left—the kitchen?; curtains tied up at their sides, bunched in the midsections as if they were leaning over and sucking in their stomachs. Through the downstairs windows he thought he saw movement, shadows skittering along the walls. The lawn sprinklers were on.

"I think this is Anna's house," Salvator said, nodding, trying to measure his luck. He tried to remember the things Nino had told him: court a woman, send her flowers. Had he said sing to her? He pointed at the Bel Air. "That's her dad's car." He paused, looked at Paulo: "Definitely."

Paulo pursed his lips. "Hmmm," he said. A smile. Paulo raised and lowered his eyebrows a couple of times, scheming. "I could sneak around back, if you want. Do a little recon. Check the lay of the land, so to speak." He was acting goofy. "Never know I was there."

Salvator looked at Paulo. Paulo did the eyebrow thing again. Salvator got out of the car and walked up the brick path towards the front doors of the house. He looked back at Paulo, who smiled and nodded and revved the Corvette's motor. Movement through the windows.

Salvator snuck up to the window closest to the front door and peaked in. There sat Toscana, roly-poly, watching television. Salvator stepped back off the tiled front porch area and walked backwards down the walkway. He looked up to the second floor windows, trying to see movement. Was this indeed Anna's house? Were they just visiting friends? He rubbed his jaw, ran his tongue around the inside of his mouth, felt the roughness on his teeth. He took in a deep breath, thought, "what the hell?" and started singing

Ho visto la luna crescente

I have seen the moon crescent

His voice broke a little; he regained control…

uno sorriso così brillante che illumina

a smile so bright it lights

and there she was, in the second floor window

il cielo freddo. Tu sei la luna crescente

cold skies. You are the moon crescent

Her eyes as big and luminous as Venus. He sang louder now, his eyes closing as love and adoration surged up in him and burst forth from his heart like water from a geyser.

*Ho visto la neve che spruzza la
terra secca*

I have seen snow sprinkle the
dry earth

He heard the front door open and saw Anna, still at the second floor window, waving her hands wildly.

E spero che tu non dai

and I hope not for you to give

Arturo Toscana wielding a bat, running towards Salvator, yelping "Get out of here!"

ma che tu sia veramente

but for you to simply be

Salvator waved to Anna, blew her a kiss, then turned and ran to the car.

Paulo, inching the car forward in an attempt to get a jump on Toscana, leaned over and unlatched the passenger's side door.

Salvator got in, winded, his face reddened. He was smiling.

"Now wasn't that worth it?" Paulo said.

Salvator ran his wrist across his mouth. Nodded. Tried to hold in a breath. Couldn't.

"I think you sing better than you cut meat," Paulo said.

Salvator shook his head. "No way." Then: "Did you see her? Isn't she the most beautiful thing you've ever seen." My Anna, my Anna! My primrose beauty! Tugger of heart strings!

They were back on the main road now, making their way to the apartment.

"She's all right."

"'All right'?" Salvator paused. "You're an idiot."

"Don't look like her pop was too happy to see you, eh?" Paulo said. "Did you see him?" Paulo laughed and shook his head. "Looked like a goddamn portly walrus trying to chase you down."

Paulo kept talking, jabbering on about how big the house was, the boat, the car—"no where near as nice as my 'Vette"—how they must waste so much water keeping that lawn green. Salvator heard little of it,

✝

his mind too full of Anna's image, there in what must have been her bedroom window. Her bedroom! Do you think of me up there, Anna? Do you find me when you look in your heart? The slim part of his mind that actually cared about Paulo's feelings urged Salvator to nod now and then show a modicum of interest when Paulo paused or raised his voice for emphasis. Salvator closed his eyes and focused his attention on Anna's visage. She hadn't smiled, now that he thought about it. Yeah, now that he thought about it, she didn't look happy to see him. He scrinched up his face, concentrating. What was that look on her face?

∼∼∼

His name was Morris Montgomery and he was a retired welder. His hair—what was left of it—was gray, and his scalp was shiny and freckled, like a polished pear. He seemed like the kind of man who lived very much in his own world, inventing realities only he could comprehend, realities only he cared about. His left eye twitched a bit when he spoke, and he spoke mostly out of the left side of his mouth. Edith, his wife, was out playing canasta with "all them women friends a hers." Morris Montgomery led Salvator into the apartment.

The apartment was very small, maybe six hundred total square feet, but it was also very clean, clearly a place Morris Montgomery took time to care about. There were four rooms, each barely large enough to hold a good sized couch. The kitchen and living room were on one side of the small hallway, entryway?, Salvator didn't know what to call it, and the bedroom and bathroom were on the opposite side. A storage closet was situated on the wall between the doors of the bedroom and the kitchen.

"Now I do my welding downstairs"—he pointed at the floor with a crusty, deformed finger—"in the garage downstairs," Morris said, rubbing the side of his nose with his forefinger. Salvator had the distinct impression he was being psychically probed, as if he were applying for a job as a top secret government agent, not trying to rent an apartment. "I won't make no noise after seven o'clock every evening, and I won't start working down there till eight in the morning. I don't work down there on Sundays, the day of my wife's lord"—he rolled his eyes—"but I do work all the other days of the week. Now I'm not in there every day, but I give you those hours just so you have an idea. Ever since I retired I been welding stuff for friends, fixing bumpers and such. Been doing some artwork too, like that bird bath you seen when you come back here. I made it."

"You're an artist?"

"Oh hell no," Morris said, pulling a stained handkerchief from his back pocket and patting the back of his neck. He blew his nose in the handkerchief, rubbed the back of his neck with it one more time, then tucked it back into his pocket. "I ain't no artsy fartsy fruitcake. Just make stuff, is all. Love to do it, so I do it. Ain't got no choice in it really."

"Eight hundred a month and that includes water and garbage?"

Morris nodded.

"And how much do you want to move in?"

"Twenty-four hundred," Morris said. "First, last, and deposit. It's a month to month rental. Ain't no lease crap. I do that case I don't like you I can kick you out."

"Sure is a nice place," Salvator said. He studied the hardwood trim around the bedroom door, the antique glass door knobs, the old one-piece kitchen countertop. "Would you take a couple more months rent up front?"

"If you're asking me will I take your money, the answer is yes I will take your money."

Salvator hedged, wondered, thought first impression, best impression, then said: "When do you think you'll know who you're going to rent it to?"

"You can have it if you want it. I already had three or four people come look at it, but none of them called back like they said they was going to, so screw 'em. I need to rent the damn place."

"You don't do that credit check thing?"

✝

"Hell no," Morris said. "I don't need some big ugly company telling me whether I got a good person or not. They ain't never met you. 'Sides, I could tell you was a good kid right off when I saw you. Don't need nobody else to tell me that. If I'm wrong, I kick you out. Simple as that." He smiled. Lots of white teeth for such a shabby guy, Salvator thought.

Salvator thought about running out to the car and asking Paulo to come in and take a look, but then he decided no, I can do this on my own. If I blow it, I blow it. "I'll take it if you'll have me," Salvator said.

They filled out the contract at the kitchen table. Salvator asked Morris for a receipt for the $4,000 in cash with which he paid. The extra two months rent would give Salvator plenty of time to find a job.

NINE

Two things rumbled in his heart: his passion for cutting meat, and his passion for Anna Toscana. Like many men whose minds fog up from the cold exterior pressure of advice from loved ones and the warm interior inertia of two consuming passions—one for a woman, the other for an art—Salvator Cavriaghi's ability to reason had been muddled. But who could reason when love was the issue?

In the last week he'd dropped a piece of meat, sliced his hand wide open, fallen in love with a girl he knew nothing about, moved out of the only house he'd ever known, gotten his own apartment, and bought a used car.

What a ruckus his life had become! For twenty-three years he'd lived the same, safe life without any disruptions. No major illnesses, no deaths of loved ones, no lost jobs or lack of money—not that they had *a lot* of money. His father and mother had always taken care of him, making sure he had everything: food on the table every night, bills paid so there'd be heat in the winter, money in his pocket from working in the shop, vacations, the experience of being responsible to a job. He'd never dated a woman—not for lack of wanting—and neither had he ever felt passion, genuine groin-twisting, heart-palpitating passion, for one. Until Anna. How many women had come and gone through the shop! And not one of them squeezed the juices from his heart like Anna. But this Anna, she

———————————— † ————————————

had floated in to the store and yanked the cork from his seriously plugged-up Passion Barrel. How his mind overflowed with thoughts of her smile and her green eyes and her voice and her scent. He'd nearly forgotten he was a butcher!

He went in to the kitchen of his new apartment and filled a cup with ice and water. Everything in the kitchen was old, from the white counter top to the painted cupboards. How many layers of paint? He'd furnished the apartment with goods from the Salvation Army—an old, stained-but-clean double bed; a musty couch he kept covered with a forest-green sheet; two matching end tables as dark as coffee; an antique, five-drawer, brass-knobbed dresser. He'd also gathered his kitchen goods from the second-hand store: a cast iron frying pan and a couple of warped but usable stainless steel pots, and two plates, two cups, two forks, two spoons and two knives, none of which matched. Paulo and a friend of his, Peter Johnson, had helped Salvator—who still had stitches in his hand—move everything into the apartment. It only took them half an hour to get everything into the rooms. Salvator wondered about the people who had previously owned his furniture. What were their stories? Why had they given up their things? Was it just junk to them? Had they moved on in their lives? Left Oakland? Had he seen any of them on Telegraph? He'd spent less than $250 on everything, but surely the original owners had spent much more.

He had nothing on the walls, no photographs or posters or artwork. He hadn't bought a kitchen table because he knew he'd be eating most of his meals on the couch in front of the television. He thought: well, if things don't fly with Anna, at least I've got this place. And then, suddenly, he felt lonely, like a singular cow in a thousand-acre field. A lot had changed in the last few weeks, none of it anything he could have predicted even two weeks ago. You can't predict the future, he thought.

Salvator went in to his bedroom and opened the last box of clothes and began stuffing them into the bottom drawer of the dresser. It was two o'clock on Friday, and he wanted very much to see Anna. She would be

✝

getting out of school in about thirty or forty minutes. If he left now, he could be to St. Joseph's, in Alameda—a twenty to thirty minute drive depending on traffic—in time to see her.

He knew going to her school could be risky. He might not be able to stop himself from singing to her, which could embarrass her in front of her friends, which could ruin his chances of ever being her husband. Husband! As if he were living a children's fairy tale. To hell with it, he thought. I've come this far.

◠◠◠

He pulled up in front of St. Joseph's, not sure how long he'd have to wait for the students to get out. After ten minutes, he couldn't stand it anymore and got out of his car and started to walk around the block of the school to see if he could see anyone in any of the classrooms. He did. He looked at his watch: 2:33. It couldn't be much longer. When he was in school, they were always out by a quarter to three.

At 2:40 a bell sounded and people started streaming from the classrooms. Hundreds of kids, all dressed in Catholic school uniforms: the boys in blue slacks, white shirts, and blue ties; the girls in blue skirts and white blouses. The girls fell into three categories of hair: long with pony tail, long in tight bun, short like the boys, whose hair, apparently, wasn't supposed to touch their starched collars. It was amazing, really, how much the students could individualize their looks in such a strictly controlled clothing environment. Those two girls, for example: one with a blouse buttoned up all the way to her throat, a skirt that reached her knees, and short hair, the other with long, frizzy hair pulled back and tied at the base of her neck with a very fluffy pink rubber band looking thing, the top two buttons of her blouse unbuttoned—this couldn't possibly be legal—and a skirt so short if she bent over she'd have to be arrested for indecent exposure. Same for the boys. Some wore ties cinched up like nooses, others, stretching the boundaries of fashion, had loosened their ties and unbuttoned the top button of

✝

their shirts. Some boys had hair like a marine sergeant, some had breached the legal limit, tendrils hanging millimeters beyond that universal measure of good boys: the collar. Some boys had earrings—Catholic schools allowed this now?—others had glasses, some had glasses and earrings.

He saw her leaving with a couple of friends near the main gate of the school. He weaved his way around the people on the sidewalk, approached her, and, when she saw him, she held up a hand and said, "Leave me alone."

"That's him?" the shorter of Anna's two friends said. She looked Salvator up and down, then rolled her eyes, as if to say "big deal."

"Anna, please," Salvator said, holding his hands up in front of him, palms facing Anna. "A moment?" He was in front of her now, walking backwards. He smiled.

She ignored him. He stopped, and the girls kept walking along the sidewalk toward the bus stop.

"Anna," he said, a little louder.

"She said leave her alone," the taller girl said, stopping and turning to face Salvator. She was a big girl, maybe six feet tall, at least a foot taller and forty pounds heavier than Anna. "So leave her alone," she said. The girl turned back and caught up with Anna and the short one.

He had no alternative. He extended his hands out in front of him, palms up this time, and closed his eyes. His voice, deep and resonant, starting in the bass:

Tu cammini delicatamente, una ballerina:
Tu, così orgogliosa, così amorevole

Gently you walk, a ballerina:
You, so proud, so lovely

The girls walking with Anna stopped and turned around. Their faces had gone pale. "That's beautiful," the shorter one said. She looked at

⸸

Anna's taller friend, said, "Lisa," and pointed with her head towards Salvator. Anna kept walking. Her friends abandoned her and walked up to Salvator.

Salvator kept singing, his voice climbing towards tenor.

> *Tutto é possibile*
> *con il tocco*
> *della tua mano*

> All is possible
> with the touch
> of your hand

He could smell basil. Then peppermint. How the hell does she do that?

> *Rosa de la mia vita*
> Rose of my life

The girls came closer. Anna kept going. Salvator started walking, slowly, in Anna's direction.

"Anna!" Lisa shouted. "How can you walk away from this? Listen to him!" Lisa turned back to Salvator. She rolled her finger at him: "Keep singing."

Now his voice doubled in volume, climbed to its operatic peak.

> *L'amore mi chiama ad*
> *amare sempre il*
> *fiore verde che*
> *avvolge il tronco*
> *del più grande albero Dio*

> Love calls me to
> love always the

         green flower that
         wraps the trunk
         of God's greatest
         tree

The song had thoroughly entranced him. His mind now utterly filled with visions of Anna. Anna on a cloud. Anna swinging. Anna dancing in a gown. Anna in his arms. Anna smiling. Anna! Oh, Anna!

Anna stopped and turned around. "Come on!" she said, glaring at her friends. "Lisa! Shelly! He's crazy." But Lisa and Shelly, their heads swaying slightly to the rhythm of Salvator's voice, did not hear.

Salvator stopped singing. "Anna," he said, ignorant of the crowd of people that had gathered behind him, most of them laughing and pointing and giggling. Some of the girls? Their knees were shaking, weakened. Other of the girls? They were weeping or nibbling on their pinkies. Some of the boys? They were scoffing, calling Salvator a "dumb ass" and a "dork." One boy—only one—was scribbling on the back of a peach colored folder, taking notes, documenting Salvator's every gesture.

"Anna," Salvator said again, "please, a moment?"

"Come on, Anna," Lisa said. "See what he has to say. We'll be right here." She stared at Salvator.

"You're as crazy as he is," Anna said, and walked around the corner.

Lisa spoke directly to Salvator: "Go get her."

Salvator smiled and nodded, "Thank you," he said. He ran to Anna and got in front of her.

She crossed her arms over her chest, stuck one foot forward, leaned her weight—which couldn't have bee more than 130 pounds—on the other leg, huffed, and looked at the sky, which was such a magnificent shade of blue Salvator thought God must have conjured a fresh set of pastels. How beautiful she makes even a Catholic uniform look, he thought. "Anna," he said. "I have fallen in love with you, and I intend to treat you tenderly and with adoration."

She shook her head. "You don't even know me. You're psycho." She had a brown leather backpack slung over her right shoulder and a green folder in her left hand. Her hair was braided in a single, long pony tail.

"Why are you being so mean, Anna?" Salvator asked. "At the hospital—"

"I don't want you around me. Period."

He didn't believe her. He couldn't believe her. She had smiled at him when he sang to her in the hospital, waved to him when he serenaded her at her house. Salvator ducked his head down, tried to see into her eyes. She just turned her head.

A boy from the crowd—which had followed them—came forward. He was big, full of muscles, with a neck like a…well, he didn't seem to have a neck. "Why don't you leave her alone," he said. He looked puffy.

Salvator ignored him. "Anna. I would like to take you out to dinner. Perhaps next week." He straightened his tie, leaned forward a little. "Please."

The boy got between Salvator and Anna. "I said leave her alone." Definitely a lot of muscles.

Salvator looked the boy in the eye. "I already do not like you and I haven't even met you."

The boy pushed Salvator and Salvator fell down. He landed on his bandaged hand, closed his eyes for a moment, then curled the hand to his chest.

"You didn't have to do that, Rich," Anna said. She knelt down next to Salvator. "Are you okay?"

He nodded.

More boys from the crowd came forward—skinny ones, fat ones, pasty ones—and stood behind Rich. "He's harassing you," Rich said.

"Leave him alone," Lisa said, pushing Rich in the chest. "He didn't do anything to you."

Anna extended a hand to Salvator and helped him up. Such softness, he thought. And strong! "Just give me a chance, Anna," he said. He brushed off his pants, smiled one last time, then turned and started walking towards his car. Behind him, he heard the murmuring of young males:

"Pathetic," he thought he heard; "weirdo," he thought he heard. He got into his car and left.

When he pulled in to the driveway at his apartment, he couldn't remember having driven there. What he did remember was the daydream: They were old, but still looked like twenty-year-olds. He was making Anna her favorite breakfast—chocolate chip pancakes from scratch, sourdough toast with butter and orange marmalade, his homemade breakfast sausage, and strong black coffee. She was still asleep in their bedroom, which, like the rest of the rooms in their little four bedroom house on their big plot of land, overlooked the Pacific Ocean somewhere in Northern California. Their eight children—John the eldest: a butcher; Isabelle the next: a doctor; Clara the next: a singer; Joe the next: a piano player; Robert the next: a teacher; Sophia the next: an actress; Angela the next: a carpenter; Dino the next: another butcher—had all grown up, gone to college, and moved out. He brought her the breakfast in bed, on a silver platter, with a silver knife, fork, and spoon. And he told her he loved her more and more each day and that they could live indefinitely on their love and his sausage.

Morris Montgomery was sweeping the driveway with a push broom. His white, v-neck T-shirt was soaked with sweat, and he looked more like a twitching bird than a man.

"How you doin' kid?" Morris said.

"Not too bad, Morris. Not too bad." Salvator smiled. He had yet to see Morris's wife, Edith, and he was beginning to wonder if Edith really existed. Morris was always by himself, and whenever he referred to her, she was elsewhere.

"She going to go out with you?" Morris said.

"What?" Salvator didn't remember telling Morris anything about Anna.

"She going to go out with you?"

"What are you talking about?"

"The girl, you idiot. Is she going to go out with you?"

"How do you know what I was doing?"

✝

"Look at you. You're sweating hormones for christsake." Morris paused. "Plus I heard about what you did yesterday, going up to Toscana's house and singing to her." Morris Montgomery laughed. "That's a good one."

"How'd you hear about that?"

"Just heard is all."

From the smell of him, Morris needed a shower. "Not yet," Salvator said. How could Morris know?

"Not yet, what?"

"Not yet, she's not going to go out with me yet."

"Send her some flowers," Morris said.

"Why?"

"What do you mean 'why'? Send her flowers. Do what I tell you."

Salvator went upstairs to his apartment. He called a local florist and ordered some flowers delivered to Anna's house.

Ten

He had his stitches out the day before, and Rose, knowing this, wanted to see her son. She'd called him in the morning and invited him over for dinner. "Your father won't be here, though," she'd said; he had work to do in his shop. Her emphasis on *his* made Salvator uneasy, as if to say he, Salvator, were no longer part of the business.

Salvator thought about going to Cavriaghi's Meats to visit his father, whom he hadn't seen or spoken to since he moved out. He decided against it. If Claudio wanted to see him, Claudio would call, and right now, Claudio was nothing but angry, and maybe a little sad—though he'd never admit *that*.

He backed the car out of the driveway and into Myrtle Lane. The nearest neighbors to Morris Montgomery's property were three hundred feet away, behind a stand of redwoods and pine and a slight ditch Morris called "the ravine." If nothing else, the apartment provided Salvator with a deep sense of solace. He'd spent the last week there nearly in shock at how absolutely silent a space could be. At his parents' house, ten minutes wouldn't go by without a siren or a car's tires screeching to a halt or a honking horn or a rumbling flock of Harley-Davidsons, their exhausts rattling the house like thunder. That's just how they lived their lives: surrounded in that most insidious kind of noise, the kind you don't even acknowledge as present until it dissipates. And now he remembered something Morris Montgomery had said the first night Salvator spent in the apartment: "Hope you like quiet." That first night was unbearable. Not only did he have Anna on his mind, and the blood on her father's car—which he still hadn't paid for—and his angry parents, he had to contend with the sheer lack of sounds. He'd tried, that first night, to make some noise for himself so he could fall asleep: he turned on the clock radio, then the television, in front of which he'd fallen asleep. But that hardly worked. He slept fitfully, waking at least once every hour, sweating, sticky, shaken. Tucked up in the woods like they were, surrounded by tall, fully needled trees, unless you created your own noise, you had to live in silence. Probably the loudest thing around the apartment, aside from his or Morris's car, were the squirrels that barked in the mornings. He had no idea squirrels sounded like nicotine-throated Chihuahuas.

Myrtle Lane dipped steeply to Snake Canyon Road, twisting to the right in one long, smooth arc. No doubt about it, this was a beautiful place. Snake Canyon Road, lined with redwoods and pines and eucalyptus, looked more like an artist's perception of reality than reality itself: twisted and drooping trees, greens and oranges and yellows that vibrated at frequencies most people never recognized. He wondered at this, Salvator did: who really took the time to notice the colors, *genuinely take note* of the colors? Like the color of light in the morning that at one moment radiated like the rinds of a trillion ripe lemons then, slowly, in increments nearly immeasurable by watches, yellow-shifted through bands of saffron and ocher and gold; or the varying degrees of oranges and reds as the sun slid down the far slope of evening. Some of the eucalyptus trunks were so white, so unbelievably *alive*, that Salvator thought they surely must give off heat.

He shifted the car into fourth gear and coasted down the long straight away before climbing again. Whoever had owned the car before him had taken good care of it. A 1983 Toyota with only 74,547 miles on it was more or less a brand new car. Everything on the car was some shade of blue, from the dark exterior paint to the lighter seats to the almost-gray-but-not dashboard. When started, the car gave off a faint odor of burning oil, but the guy who sold it to Salvator, Mickey Schneider, assured him the smell came from a few drops of oil he'd dripped on the manifold during the oil change he'd performed the evening before Salvator bought the car.

It was only six o'clock. The sun still had nearly three hours left in Oakland's sky, its beams streaming through the trees like tangerine fingers.

At the stop light at the end of Snake Canyon Road, Salvator turned left into Mountain Boulevard, the four-lane, traffic clogged street that served as the main line into Montclair. If he'd have turned right, he'd have driven into Montclair's miniature downtown: a couple of two laned streets lined with shiny new coffee houses, realtors, bagel shops, a sporting goods store, a couple of pizza joints, and other shops filled with crafts or hardware or photography equipment. He felt out of place in his little blue car. Many of the people living in Montclair drove luxury cars or sport-utility vehicles or luxury sport-utility vehicles.

He turned right on Park Boulevard, then left to get on to Highway 13. From this point, Highway 13 hooked upwards and to the left, like the long talon of a gargantuan, mile-high raptor. As he exited the freeway, he had the notion swilling around in the bottom of his brain that he'd like his mother to look a little weathered, a little more wrinkled since he'd left. He shook it off: ridiculous. She'd look exactly the same, if not better since he moved out. Maybe his absence gave her back a few years.

Nothing about the house looked different as he pulled in to the driveway: the same green juniper, the same green paint, the same green tree, the same green ivy. Everything the same as he'd left it. Absolutely the same as it'd always been and always would be.

She answered the door wearing a bright red sweat suit. He could smell hot olive oil and beef cooking in it: she'd cooked his favorite dinner, breaded meat. Nothing, no single thing in the universe—except maybe her meatballs—could compare to those thin flank steaks dipped in oil then rolled in her seasoned bread crumbs and fried in her cast iron skillet.

It was scientifically impossible for any other food—except maybe her meatballs—to taste that good. Salvator inhaled deeply.

Her first words: "You need a haircut."

"I know," Salvator said. This bush they'd beaten around a thousand times, both of them thinking the other one was out of line.

They headed towards the kitchen. He could hear the meat sizzling in the pan. Rose ripped open a bag of frozen French fries and tossed them in with the last two pieces of meat. "Another minute. Go wash."

They sat down to eat. Salvator heaped his plate with three slices of breaded meat, a pile of salad, and a mound of French fries. He squirted ketchup over the fries and ate a few to start. Normally, at any other meal, Salvator was a one-at-a-time eater. He'd eat all of his salad first, then move, say, to the steak, then eat the potatoes, or whatever. But when he had to contend with a plate of his mother's breaded meat, a fine balance had to be reached in his mouth. The meat had to be dipped into the ketchup on top of the fries and, for most of the bites, he had to skewer a fry or two on his fork while soaking the meat in the ketchup. This after swirling the meat in a little of the vinegar and oil dressing pooled beneath the salad. A very delicate operation.

He swigged down a mouthful of root beer. "So where's dad? He still mad at me?"

Rose snorted. "Yes."

"Are you still mad at me?"

"Yes."

"Then why'd you cook me dinner?"

"You *are* my son, even though you're stupid. You get that from your father."

She definitely did not look any more wrinkled. If anything, she'd taken on an even feistier glare. She looked at him as if he smelled bad.

Rose said, "He's going to sell."

Salvator drew his head back, chewed.

"They raised the offer to $750,000," she said, "so he took it."

✝

Salvator put his fork down and swallowed. *Unbelievable*, he thought. "When did this happen?" Salvator said.

"Three days ago."

"Why didn't you guys call me?"

"Why should we call you?" Rose set her napkin on the table. "I'm telling you now."

"Oh Jesus."

She turned around. "What did you say?"

"I said 'Oh Jesus.' It's not like I said 'fuck' or something like that."

Rose inhaled deeply. "I'm letting that go, Salvator, because I didn't ask you over here to get into it with you."

Miracle of miracles, he thought. Salvator reached over and plopped another slice of meat on his plate. He thought: I can piss her off or I can stay calm. He let a long breath out through his mouth, silently. His breath stank. He raised his eyebrows and pursed his lips. "So when does he get the money?" he said.

"I don't know," Rose said. She started washing the dishes, which she always did halfway between her meals.

"What are you guys going to do, fix up the back room like you been thinking?"

"We're moving."

Salvator considered cursing out loud again. "What?"

"As soon as the money comes in we're putting the house up. You know how we used to go up to Arcata and Eureka for our summer trip, go to the redwoods? Well, for a long time now he's wanted to get a small place in the woods, away from the city—"

"Since when?" Salvator said. "He never said anything about that to me. Neither did you."

"We don't tell you everything, Salvator."

Salvator shook his head. "So he's just giving up? Is that it?"

"I don't think working over thirty years in his own shop is giving up."

"What am I supposed to do?"

"You're a big boy. You'll be fine."

"What about Paulo and Nino? What about them?"

"He's going to give them each $50,000 so they can have some time to rest and find more work. Nino said he might move north too, maybe find a place near where we move."

By the time Rose finished the first round of dishes, Salvator had finished his meal. He did his own dishes, knowing while he did them that she'd rewash them. They sat down on the couch and drank coffee. Rose talked about moving, about Claudio finally giving in to the "corporate assholes." She talked about how, once they'd decided to take the money, they felt like they were breathing again after a long period of breathlessness. Salvator listened, nodded a lot, mused on visiting them, lamented them leaving the home he grew up in. "It's just a house," she'd said at one point. "And it's falling apart anyway."

She asked about Anna, even said "she's a nice girl," which Salvator took as a veiled "I approve, but don't tell your father."

They were standing on the front walk, Rose with her arms folded, Salvator a few steps in front of her, hands on his hips, his tongue trying to work a chunk of meat out from behind one of his molars. He'd hoped to stay long enough that his father would have to come home, but by eight-thirty Salvator realized, without Rose having to say so, that Claudio would not show up until Salvator left. "I can't believe you guys are going to sell this place," he said.

"It's not the building that's important," she said. "It's the people that live in it." She stared at him. "We've done a lot of living in this house. A lot. Raised you. Kept a business going. Those kinds of things don't stay in a house when you sell it, Salvator. They go with you."

Salvator tilted his head to the right, then to the left, stretching the sides of his neck. He didn't entirely agree. A house, especially one like this one, one a family has lived in for nearly thirty years, well, a house like that was part of the family, like the comforting uncle who takes you out camping, or the aunt that pinches your cheeks every time she sees you. "I don't know," he said. "I'm not so sure that's true. I mean, this house has been here for us, just like we've been here for each other."

"House burns down," she said, "everything in it burns down. What do you have left? Family. That's it. That's all you have in this world, Salvator. Me and your father. Nobody else. We're the ones who love you."

"What about Nino? And Paulo? Don't you consider them family?" He thought for a moment. "And your brothers and sisters?"

"They're all family. And you don't need a house in Oakland for them to stay family. They will always be family." She stepped towards the front door and pushed open the screen door. He'd never heard his mother talk like this, never knew she thought like this. For years he'd sensed her happiness waning, though he'd never doubted her love for him and his father. She was a woman after all, and he couldn't help but think that for her the idea of moving north was a way for to recapture some romance with her husband. "I'll tell your father you said hello."

As he drove past the blackened-by-night trees of Snake Canyon Road, he felt as though he had a boulder on his shoulder. If he'd have just stayed home and not moved out, his parents wouldn't be moving. They wouldn't be giving up everything they'd worked so many years to build. The house, the shop, their family. If he'd have loved his parents rather than Anna, if he'd have respected their decisions, this wouldn't be happening. But *they* had decided to move, not him. It had been their decision.

Salvator knew, too, the truth of it: if his parents said they were moving, then they were moving. Period. Neither of them would joke about a thing like that or even bring it up as a possibility if in fact it wasn't already a plan. Claudio was a man of his word, with enough strength of will and character that anyone, from his closest relative to a complete stranger, could depend on one of his promises.

Salvator remembered a time when he was sixteen years old, and he and his father got into a fight. That particular day, Salvator was tired of being a butcher. "I want to sing," he'd said, sweeping up around the shop. He was "sick of all the goddamn meat."

"What did you say?" Claudio had said. They were standing near the open door of the cold storage. Cold air and the smell of frozen meat eddied around their ankles. His father's head was cocked sideways and thrust forward, like a bird listening to an awkward sound. He was squinting, and he cupped his left hand up to his left ear, "Say it again, what you said. I don't think I heard you."

"I said I'm sick of all the goddamn meat and these dumbshit knives," Salvator said, smacking the palm of his hand against the scabbard on his hip and thrusting his chin forward. Salvator stared right into his father's eyes. By that time Salvator stood two inches taller than Claudio—half a mile in Salvator's mind—and he outweighed his dad by ten pounds.

"What kind of meat?" Claudio said.

Salvator took two steps back. He said it slowly, and through his teeth: "God…damn…meat. That kind."

"I hear you're quite a butcher already, Salvator." Salvator and Claudio spun around. They hadn't heard the customer, Father Bartolucci, come in. The priest leaned at the display case. Unlike other Catholic priests, Father Bartolucci rarely wore the standard black uniform and white band when he was away from the rectory, and that day, as he stood there, smiling at Salvator and his father, he wore blue jeans and a green button down shirt with hiking boots. If he was seen wearing his "priest's get-up," as he called it, you usually knew one of two things: he'd either gotten in trouble again and had a meeting with the bishop—usually for "not conducting himself in a priestly manner"—or he was going to administer last rites to a dying person.

"Hello, Father," Claudio said as he approached the priest. "I didn't hear you come in."

The two men shook hands, firmly, over the counter. Father Bartolucci said, looking at Salvator and nodding towards Claudio, "You know, he brags about you at the parish board meetings."

✝

Salvator started sweeping again. "Big deal." Back then, in his "rebellious teens" as his mother always referred to them, Salvator had no qualms about speaking his mind.

"Big deal?" Father Bartolucci said. He laughed. "He's proud of you, you big dummy."

Salvator smiled.

"Come here," Father Bartolucci said.

Salvator exhaled, dramatically, as if Father Bartolucci had asked him to do the imponderable, like wear pink underwear or pick his nose at a prom. He didn't move, but he did stop sweeping and look right at the priest. "He wants me to be a butcher. What if I don't want to be a butcher? What if I want to play music? I'm a good singer."

"Then go be a singer," Father Bartolucci said.

Claudio's face wrinkled up as if he'd smelled something rotten. He rubbed his eyes with the forefinger and thumb of his right hand. "Father!" he said through his teeth, "I hope you know what you're doing."

The priest nodded his response but kept his eyes on Salvator. Now he looked at Claudio. "Can I step back there and talk to him?"

"Of course," Claudio said.

Father Bartolucci approached Salvator and extended his hand. Salvator took it, limp, sensing a set up.

"Look," Father Bartolucci said, "he loves you. You know that. He's just doing the best he can. You know that, too. So why break his heart? Why give up—"

"Why? I'm not him," Salvator said, raising his voice a little. He looked over to where his father had been standing, but Claudio had moved to the other side of the display case, out of hearing range. He was fiddling with the boxes of plastic liners they used to cover the meat when they wrapped it. "He *wanted* to be a butcher," Salvator said. "I'm not so sure *I* want to be one."

"Have you ever *worked* as a musician? Do you have any idea how hard those people work? Do you know the hours?" Father Bartolucci pointed at the wooden plank floor. "Here, if you have something important to do, he'll give you the time off, whenever you need it. Right?" Salvator nodded. "If you work playing music, especially if you're just starting out, you won't get to do that. You'll work twenty-four hours a day. Trust me. Plus, he tells everybody he's never seen anyone cut meat the way you do. You should see him at those meetings. It takes us ten minutes just to shut him up so we can get started!"

Salvator smiled again.

"Look, you're what, sixteen now? Believe me, I know the feelings you're having. My father was a farmer in North Dakota—"

"And now you're a priest. You're not a farmer."

Father Bartolucci touched Salvator's shoulder. "Salvator," he said. "My father knew I'd be a priest long before I ever did. He told me once—I was about your age now, maybe a year younger—he said, 'John, you know nothing about farming. You can't fix the tractor, you can't plow a straight line,' this is what he told me, he said, 'I just want you to know it's okay. Go be a priest.' I thought he was nuts! Five years later"—Father Bartolucci snapped his fingers—"I was in the seminary."

"I don't mean no offense, Father, but what does this have to do with me?"

"Father's know, Salvator. They know in their bones what their sons are good at. They know that better than they know what they want out of their own lives. Your dad has given you your art. The way he talks, you must love cutting meat. He makes it sound like your God's personal butcher!"

Salvator bounced his head from side to side, shrugged his shoulders.

"Just think about it before you throw in the towel, okay?"

Salvator grunted and went back to sweeping.

Father Bartolucci winked to Claudio on his way out.

"So what'd he say?" Claudio asked, his voice soft now, loving, the same voice a father gets the first time he teaches his son how to use a wrench.

Salvator looked at his father then looked away. "He said you brag about me. He said you think I'm a better butcher than you are."

†

Claudio stuck out his lower lip. "That's what he said, huh?" Claudio turned and walked toward his block. "He drinks too much wine"—a pause: he turned to face Salvator—"When you're done sweeping, I need you to sharpen my knives."

Now Salvator stood on the steps of the new apartment. His mother had mentioned that business had suffered since Salvator left the shop, that customers who wanted Salvator to cut their meat just stopped coming in.

He walked in and slumped down on the couch. Last year some time Paulo had been telling Salvator about his practice of Ninpo, how in that art one of the most important things for the beginning practitioner to understand was the importance of balance. Balance in all aspects of one's life. Physical balance when standing or walking or sitting or fighting; emotional and spiritual balance when meditating. Paulo had described it as "ura" and "omote," the inner and outer aspects of life, and he'd told Salvator that he, Salvator, had to realize that everything in life could not possibly be all good or all bad, and that if a person feels like things are going extremely well in his or her life, then that person needs to acknowledge the shadow side of life, acknowledge the possibility that too much goodness must be balanced with some shadow. As he thought this through, Salvator wondered if perhaps Anna entering his life had been some kind of balancing effect, a way for the Cosmos to let Salvator know that to have her in his life, for her to bring lightness and goodness and love to him, he would have to experience some darkness, and that darkness, that balancing effect manifested itself in his parents' decision to move away. Familial love to amore. Adolescence to manhood. These paths, Paulo had told him, were treacherous and beautiful, and even the mightiest of warriors faced untold difficulties trying to navigate them.

ELEVEN

"Bless me Father for I think I have sinned," Salvator said.

"Salvator?"

"Yes Monsignor. It has been one week—"

"I know, I know," Monsignor Jackson said. "What time is it?"

Salvator looked at his watch in the dim light of the confessional. Salvator's voice, flaccid: "Five minutes to six."

"Then you're my last sinner." The Monsignor laughed. A door unlatched in the Monsignor's cubby. "Let's go back to the rectory. I want some coffee."

Set off from the church by fifty-feet, the rectory, finished in the same beige stucco and scalloped terra-cotta roof tile as the church, looked professionally manicured. Part of the weekly collection went to grounds keeping on the church's premises. Between the church and rectory stretched an awning-covered walkway lined with rose bushes. The rectory itself was surrounded by a lawn so finely mowed in some places that Monsignor Jackson could practice putting, which he did, every day, right after 7:00 a.m. mass. Against the wall of the rectory, filling a space maybe three feet wide, a juniper hedge trimmed to three feet in height. The hedge seemed so square and thick to Salvator, he often wondered if it was fake. In front

✝

of the hedge, butted up against the lawn, assorted flowers in various shades of yellow and red and white and purple.

Salvator and the Monsignor walked side-by-side, in silence, to the rectory. Monsignor Jackson, his priest's clothing stuck to his body with sweat, had done this before with Salvator. At least once each month—Salvator confessed his sins weekly—the Monsignor would generate some reason to leave the church's cherry-wood lined confessionals and have Salvator confess the minutiae of his soul face to face. The excuses ranged from "too cramped in here," to "haven't seen you in a while"—which was always untrue, considering Salvator, for the last ten years, had never missed mass or confession—to "coffee, I need some coffee." Monsignor Jackson—he'd been Father Jackson when he first came to St. Peter's—liked to "mix it up," as he'd say, when it came to Salvator's penance. Sometimes Salvator would get ten Hail Marys and five Our Fathers, other times, the reverse. Even the occasional Act of Contrition, if he felt it necessary, would sneak into the Monsignor's repertoire. Occasionally Monsignor Jackson would ask Salvator to say a complete rosary, like the time Salvator admitted to then-Father Jackson that he, Salvator, had taken $500 in payment from a man for painting the man's garage. Salvator didn't claim the money on his taxes; he'd just taken the job—he only did it once—because he wanted some extra cash to help Claudio pay off a loan on the display case that was now over ten years old. "Sins like these," Father Jackson had said behind the withering screen of the confessional, "they will not get you time in Purgatory if you genuinely repent for them now. Say a rosary in front of the Blessed Virgin, tell her you're sorry, and mean it."

Inside the air-conditioned rectory, Monsignor Jackson pointed to the pine table and chairs in the kitchen and suggested Salvator have a seat. "You look terrible," Monsignor Jackson said, pointing to Salvator's misbuttoned and untucked shirt. "I heard about the hand. How's it doing?" The Monsignor poured himself and Salvator some coffee.

"Fine."

The Monsignor was a giant man—you could fit Salvator in his belly, it seemed—with a voice as deep and loud as a tired fog horn. He had the blackest skin Salvator had ever seen, and his eyes bulged from their caverns like spherical buoys surfacing on the flat plane of an ocean. In three more months, Monsignor Jackson would celebrate his sixtieth birthday. "Halfway," he would say, "to one-twenty." His drive to live well through the second decade of his second century was as unflappable as his devotion to God. And everyone believed he'd do it, despite the strain his colossal dimensions surely placed on his heart.

"So, Salvator, you *think* you've sinned?" Monsignor Jackson gulped down some coffee. "That's a new one." The edges of his lips glistened with sweat.

"Monsignor," Salvator said. He rubbed his forehead with his hand and looked up at the ceiling. "I think I've dishonored my father and mother."

Monsignor Jackson rolled his eyes. "What did you do?"

Salvator explained everything that had happened over the course of the last couple of weeks. Monsignor Jackson listened, every so often taking a sip of his coffee. When Salvator got to the point about his feelings for Anna, he bit down on his lower lip and looked down at his coffee mug. He fiddled with its handle and said, "Monsignor"—a pause—"I have urges."

The Monsignor took a deep breath, leaned back in his chair, and covered his thick face with his thicker hands. "Urges," he said.

"Yes, Monsignor. I can think only of Anna, and mostly I think of how beautiful she is and how much I'd like to, well"—Salvator wagged his hand in the air.

Monsignor Jackson raised his eyebrows and, slightly, tilted forward in his chair. "How old is this girl, Salvator?"

"She is seventeen."

The Monsignor twisted his mug around and laughed at the cartoon on it: two dogs scratching the belly of a man, the man's leg fluttering from the tickle. Salvator stared at the Monsignor. Monsignor Jackson nodded, solemn, waved his hand a little. "The Catholic Church teaches us that a

✝

man and woman should not"—he waved his hand exactly the same way Salvator had a moment before—"until they are married. The Oakland Police teach us that they arrest people who commit statutory rape."

I'm screwed, whatever I do, Salvator thought.

Monsignor Jackson creaked back in his chair, lifting its front legs off the ground. He laced his fingers on top of his head, his arms forming two massive greater-than signs, as if everything his elbows pointed at—the rest of the world—amounted to less than the contents of his mind. It could be true. He already had three Ph.Ds—one in philosophy, one in comparative religions, and one in theology—and he was currently working on his fourth at the University of California at Berkeley: psychology. He'd finished his theological dissertation at a Jesuit seminary in late 1972 after returning from Viet Nam. "Well," he said, "you're a young, virile man, and having those urges you're talking about is perfectly natural. Every man has had them."

"Even you?"

"I'm a man," Monsignor Jackson said. "But I choose celibacy because of my devotion to God."

"So what should I do?"

"The least you can do, Salvator, is honor this girl and wait until she turns eighteen before you try anything sexual. And then, if you can do it, wait until you marry her. This, of course, assumes that"—the Monsignor pointed in the general direction of Salvator's crotch—"you can wait that long."

"Would I go to hell if I only kissed her?"

Monsignor Jackson pulled his chair up next to Salvator and laid his battleship-sized arm around Salvator's shoulders. "Salvator," he said, "I do not believe God would damn to hell two young people who genuinely love each other. But you must genuinely love each other. How can you possibly love this girl after knowing her for such a short time? She hardly knows you!" He paused, leaned back in his chair, a little winded. "Go slowly, Salvator. Give yourself some time to *fall* in love."

✝

They talked on longer—drinking two more pots of coffee—comparing and contrasting the different scenarios Salvator faced: his parents moving away, his feelings for Anna, how his love felt divided between the passion he had for a woman and the respect he had for his parents. In the end, after nearly three hours of good talk with the good Monsignor, Salvator left the rectory knowing that the greatest step from childhood to manhood was the infinite leap a boy had to make in *recognizing* himself as a man.

TWELVE

By the end of March of the following year, Claudio and Rose had moved to their small, two-bedroom house on six-acres of land in the town of Trinidad, three-hundred-some-odd miles and six hours north of Oakland. In an effort to sell their house quickly, they deliberately listed it for ten percent less than the average selling price of other homes in the area, and it worked. They had a buyer within forty-three days of putting it on the market. Salvator's relationship with his parent's had, over the intervening months, become more and more strained. He'd tried, on Monsignor Jackson's advice, to mend the break with his father—even Rose had grown somewhat tired of it—by offering to help Claudio dismantle Cavriaghi's Meats, but, quite to Salvator's surprise, Claudio's anger only swelled, until, in one final shouting match—Claudio shouting out his disgust for "puny young men who think they know every damn thing about how to live a life," Salvator shouting back his distaste for "old, balding men in a mid-life crisis who think they know every damn thing about every one else's life"—he, Salvator, refused to help them pack, refused to help them lug old furniture to the Salvation Army, refused, even, to have a last supper with them. Claudio had made it perfectly clear: if Salvator insisted on pursuing Anna, Claudio insisted Salvator not come around anymore. Their wills butted up against each other like two rams battling over territory, neither of them willing to accept defeat.

✝

From the time he'd first met Anna almost seven months ago, his love
for her had daily intensified, finally sending him over the brink of
infatuation into the pool of obsession—he had, within four months of
first seeing her in the shop, mailed or covertly delivered to Anna a total
of fourteen hand-picked bouquets of flowers, nineteen love letters, six
pounds of chocolate fudge in half-pound boxes, thirty-seven poems,
and serenaded her forty-two times. Yes, he had done all of these things
and done them all with nothing but genuine love in his heart—he
remembered the Monsignor's words—but by the beginning of the new
year, when he finally began to realize that no matter what he did, no matter how romantic or daring or chivalrous his gestures were, they would be
met with either Anna's dismissal, her mother's anger, or her father's inde-
fatigable fury, he slowly ended his reign of adoration, and, by the first
Saturday in February, brought to an end all contact with Anna.

Once, deep into Salvator's campaign, Arturo Toscana had called the
cops on him, and the cops just gave Salvator a warning. When Toscana
heard that Salvator hadn't stopped, that Salvator was still bothering Anna
at school and at basketball games and even at the mall when she went
shopping, Arturo Toscana filed a restraining order against Salvator. This,
when he reflected upon it, Salvator acknowledged as the turning point.

It was both because of the restraining order and the fact that he hadn't
bothered her at all in nearly two months that Salvator was surprised to
find the envelope with Arturo Toscana's return address wedged in the jamb
of his front door. The envelope was thin. Salvator's name, without his
address, was typed in the center. No stamp or postmark. Someone—and
not someone from the Post Office—had delivered it. What now, he
thought. He stood there on the little wooden stoop, the chill air—or was
it the envelope—covering him in goose flesh. He opened it.

> *Meet me behind the gym at half-time during the*
> *basketball game next Friday.*   *Anna*

✝

His heart, followed by his lungs, leapt up out of his mouth, ran down the stairs, and did a little jig in the driveway. He covered his face with the letter and let out a yelp. This he could never have predicted. Never ever never ever never *never*. Talk about a turn of luck, a jackpot, a bonanza, a blessing, a big fat double-scoop-with-chocolate-sauce surprise! Somehow, he surely didn't know how, he figured out how to unlock the front door with the keys in his pocket. He danced around his apartment singing arias that, this time, probably *did* wake Caruso from his infinite nap.

Within an hour, after much paranoid deliberation with himself, he was convinced that it was a set-up by Arturo Toscana. He went back and forth with it for another half an hour, then finally decided to enlist Paulo's help.

He reached Paulo at home. Together, they decided that the best plan of action would be to send one of Paulo's trusty friends in Salvator's place. If the meeting was legitimate, the friend of Paulo's would give Anna a note from Salvator with words she'd recognize from one of the love poems he'd sent her, and another place and time to meet. If the meeting was indeed a set-up, then the guy could just say he'd stepped out back to have a cigarette and no one would know the difference.

It turned out that the meeting was not a set-up by Arturo Toscana and that Anna did indeed want to meet with Salvator, though she refused to tell the friend why. She scheduled the next meeting for the next home game, one week later.

What unbelievable pressure to wait another week! What does she want? What will she wear? What will she smell like? Oh! He could hardly breathe.

He scarcely slept that week, staying up late at night, cleaning the already clean apartment, doing loads of laundry even when he only had a pair of pants and a pair of underwear to wash. He was so saturated with adrenaline—and anxiety—that he had no choice but to keep busy. He would go in to work—he'd gotten the job cutting meat at the Safeway a mile up the street from his dad's shop just a few months earlier—an hour early each morning and stay, willingly, and without pay, for two to three hours beyond his scheduled off time. He cut and trimmed so much meat

✝

that week that his boss, Bud Gardner, had to tell him to stop because they didn't have enough counter space to store it all. Gardner, an old, white-haired, scab-knuckled butcher long ago transplanted from his father's farm in Western New York, already knew of Salvator—what butcher these days didn't?—and had hired him on the spot when Salvator came in and asked for work.

The night before the Day of Reckoning, Salvator asked Gardner if he could have the day off, and Gardner told Salvator to take two days, that it was no problem, he'd get the rest of the guys to cover for him.

∼∼∼

Salvator woke at 10:23 a.m., an hour after he'd collapsed on his bed, fully clothed. He'd spent the entire night fretting over what he'd say to Anna—I love you! Marry me! My little orange butterfly!—considering what he'd wear to see Anna—a suit? a tuxedo? tennis shoes and blue jeans?—pondering how he'd approach her—timidly? shyly? shaking?: God forbid, sweating?—writing her a short love poem, and puzzling over what she'd say to him—Leave me alone! I love you, too! Oh how this last one rattled every one of his cells right down to their nuclei, made the marrow in his bones shiver. She couldn't be telling me to leave her alone. I haven't bugged her for weeks. It must be love! It can only be love!

Over the course of the day, Salvator vomited three times, had four bowel movements, and, wanting to call her, picked up the phone and dialed the first *six* digits of her telephone number twelve times. His palms were sweating, and every square inch of his skin had its own unique itch. After going on a four and half mile walk down and back up Snake Canyon Road, Salvator took his third shower for the day. He could have used twelve bars of soap and rubbed anti-perspirant all over his palms, but they refused to stop sweating.

He finally opted to wear blue jeans and a plain, forest-green T-shirt so as not to draw too much attention to himself. He decided against bringing

†

her flowers for the same reasons. He folded the love poem he'd written for her and tucked it in to his back pocket.

She was waiting for him when he arrived. Her friend—Lisa was it?—saw him first. She pointed at Salvator, leaned over and said something into Anna's ear, then turned and went back in to the gymnasium.

Salvator could see into some of the cars in the lot. In one car: a young couple making out. In another: an old man, a father or grandfather, waiting, asleep, his white-capped head cocked backwards, mouth wide open. There was a group of three boys at the far end of lot, laughing, their black leather jackets catching the light of one of the street lamps.

He waved to Anna, a limp wave, timid. *No! Not timid!* He straightened his back, tried—with little success—to stick out his chest. Oh how he wanted to sing!

Anna didn't get up from her place on the concrete steps. She just looked at him: a faint smile.

He sat down next to her and he could feel the weight of the Solar System in his chest and his heart racing like a slapped-ass-and-scared horse and him wanting badly to sing to her, to kneel down and just plain belt one out loud enough so the folks yelling and happy and playing and cheering inside the gym could hear.

The buzzer sounded, muffled a bit by the rooting fans.

"Hi," she said.

"Hi," he said. He bit down on his lower lip.

"So you're probably wondering why I wanted to see you."

He smiled and nodded. "I probably am," he said. Man did she smell good. And she looked elegant in the long mahogany-colored, velvety dress. He felt dizzy. Thin white sandals, the painted toe-nails—he couldn't make out the color in the light: dark though, no doubt about that. "I thought about not coming," he said, not knowing why he said it because he'd never thought it.

She cocked her head to the side.

"I don't know," he said. "I mean, well," he hiked up his shoulders and flipped his hands up. "I don't know what to say. I'm very happy to see you."

"I'm happy to see you, too, Salvator," she said. And when she smiled and tilted her head down like that he thought: well, I'm going to die now. God is definitely going to take me this time because she's going to break my heart. "I have something I want to say to you, Salvator, so I'm just going to say it, okay?"

The muscles in his body stiffened. He could not nod.

"Okay," she said, brushing her hands down along the sides of her thighs a few quick times. "I'm just going to say it. I told myself I'd say it," she looked at her feet, "so I'm going to say it." Her chin touched the top of her chest; she took a deep breath: "I love you, Salvator."

Salvator smiled and took her left hand in his right. How warm and smooth and precious! She wrapped her right hand over the top of their clasped hands, then proceeded to tell Salvator about how flattered she'd been to have so many songs sung to her, how the flowers made her giddy, how she'd never had a boy, let alone a man with his own apartment, try so hard to win her heart. She explained how she had to put on the angry face towards Salvator because her father absolutely despised him and forbade her from seeing him.

Salvator wept and began to sing to her in a whispery lullaby-voice. He told her that he never knew she felt for him as he did for her. That she should become an actress, she makes her anger so real! He told her that now he would know, the angrier she looked the more he knew she loved him, and the greater his smile would be. It would become their secret code, he said.

She stopped him there, said no, it will not be our code because I am tired of hiding my feelings for you, because I miss your attention, because I don't want my father to ruin what makes me happy. "No," she said, "we will not have a secret code because I am going to tell my father how I feel about you. And I'm going to ask him to drop the restraining order."

"When are you going to do this?" Salvator said.

✝

"I don't know," Anna said. She crossed her arms, stood, and rubbed her elbows. "But I'm going to."

"I don't want you to get in to trouble," Salvator said. "I'm six years older than you, and that's a huge difference when you're just seventeen. Your father has every right—"

"My father is nothing," she said. She looked up at a street lamp in the parking lot.

The buzzer sounded again.

"I have to go in," Anna said. "Meet me here, same time next week." She bent down, kissed Salvator on the cheek, and walked in to the gym. The crowd's roar: louder now as she opened the door.

THIRTEEN

Salvator spent the next week in la-la land, singing to himself, singing to strangers on the street, singing to his car as he washed and waxed it, singing thank yous to customers at the Safeway meat counter. An angry customer? *Sir, I apologize for the mistake*—he'd wrung up two tenderloins instead of one, his mind being otherwise occupied—*and I will pay for a second tenderloin, giving you two for the price of one.* The rust on his car? *What beautiful bubbles*! He even called his parents and spoke to his mother, who sounded happy to hear from him and hear his news, even though she yelled at him and told him he was "stupid" and "crazy." He helped old ladies across the street. He gave a free lecture at work for interested customers: "How to Sharpen Your Knives by Salvator Cavriaghi, Butcher" (So many people showed up for this—nearly three hundred!—Bud Gardner, laughing like a six-year-old who just learned what the word "poop" means, had to turn people away.) Each day of the week, Salvator wrote Anna a new love song. He'd write her a song a day for the rest of her life! He'd sing her to sleep, sing to wake her up, he'd sing to their children and grandchildren!

But Anna wasn't behind the gym when he showed up.

Lisa was.

Salvator walked up to Lisa, smiling. "Where's Anna?" he said. He flicked a thumb in the direction of the gym's door. "She still in there?" Then the look on Lisa's face registered with him: Anna was not inside.

As Lisa explained to Salvator how Anna had told her father how she felt and that her father didn't take it very well and that Arturo had beaten Anna up enough to give her a black eye and a sprained finger and Anna didn't want Salvator to see her like that and—as she went on with this, Salvator sucked in his lips, tensed up his face. Hands at his sides, he made fists, released them. He wanted badly to know Paulo's art of self-defense. He nodded as Lisa continued on, though he was hardly listening, hearing only snippets, key words: "…loves you…," "…see you again…." Salvator rubbed the back of his neck, took in a long and deep breath.

When Lisa stopped, he said, "How long has this been going on?" And before she could answer: "I remember the first time I saw her, when she took me to the hospital, I saw a bruise on her arm."

Lisa nodded. "It's nothing new, Salvator."

He nodded. Stopped listening while Lisa talked on. Something in him clicked, a recognition of sorts, as if a switch in his mind had been toggled, his unconscious mind trying to complete a circuit with his conscious perception. He felt suddenly cold, an unexpected and discomfiting sensation, like the chill he'd felt, years and years before, when his father, in one of those moments weighed down by history, explained to him how his blood was the blood of his ancestors, those dilapidated Sicilian farmers constantly ransacked by malevolent tyrants, those "good farmers" whose skin, Claudio had said, "was as hard and taut as hammered metal."

Salvator thanked Lisa and drove straight to Anna's house. He parked down the street and walked up to the house. The light was on in her bedroom, and he thought he saw, through the yellow curtains, her silhouette. To his right: Toscana's Chevrolet. Salvator wanted badly to kick a dent into the driver's side door. He didn't. From where he stood on the sidewalk at the edge of the Toscana lawn, he could see into the living room on the downstairs floor, and he could see the fuzzy light of a reading lamp, and he could see the bluish flickering glow of a television set. And he could see, bulging over the back of the couch a shape like a bloated scrotum, the fat head of Arturo Toscana. *Dirt*! Salvator spat on the Toscana walkway. He strode to the front door, banged on it, then stepped back about ten steps onto the lawn, just out of reach of the porch light when it came on. He looked up to see Anna looking down at him. Arturo Toscana opened the door, saw Salvator, and charged him.

Salvator stood his ground and took the full force of Toscana's tackle. It nearly knocked the wind out of him. As Salvator tried to wriggle free, Toscana slapped and punched his face. Toscana's voice, loud, cracking and inarticulate, garbled words: "my dotta! alone! sunnabitch!" Salvator tasted blood in his mouth.

Somehow, Salvator's right foot drew up under Toscana's belly. Salvator pushed hard, and Toscana rolled off of him, giving Salvator enough time to scramble free and sprint. He ran, not looking back, in the direction opposite of where he'd parked his car. Toscana chased him for about a minute, screeching obscenities and curses.

When he was certain Toscana had given up, Salvator, his heart pounding, slowed to a walk, slowed some more, then stopped and bent over, propping his hands on his knees. He was winded, no doubt, both physically and emotionally. He sat down on the curb, near where he'd stopped running, and rested his head in his hands. A squadron of emotions bombarded him: anger at Toscana, then exhilaration for getting away, then frustration at feeling powerless, and longing to see Anna, and finally, his heart's last sortie for the night, a sinking sadness.

He wiped his mouth, then looked at his hand. Blood. He saw the scar in his palm, a thick, pale ridge.

That Toscana, he thought. What a bastard. He shook his head. He didn't know how a man could hurt a young girl, didn't know how a man like that could live with himself. What have I done but given her pain? Had she lived her entire life like this? Lisa's words came back to him: "nothing new." What drives a man to hit his own daughter? Then more

✝

vile thoughts. Had Toscana done worse? Abused her in other, more horrible ways?

Salvator stood and walked back in the direction of his car. He crossed the street when he came to Anna's block. He stood there for a moment and looked at her house. There were no lights on.

FOURTEEN

He woke the next morning with a sore face. The cut on his lower lip ached, as did his right eye, though they were not as swollen as they felt. He made himself some sausage, toast, and coffee for breakfast, and sat down on his couch to eat. He remembered he'd dreamed during the night, but now, sitting there eating his food, he couldn't remember at all what he'd dreamed about.

He wanted badly to speak to his father, to call him and talk to him and ask him for advice, to mend their friendship, but the rift between them was now over four months old and he doubted seriously that his father would even acknowledge him as his son. This thought made him feel terrible, and he set the half-eaten plate of food on the coffee table. After all, Salvator walked out on the family. Just up and left. He missed his parents. And now, mingling with the feelings precipitated by last night's events were the feelings of guilt he'd stuffed away and tried to forget.

He wondered what Anna was doing right now. What had Toscana done to her last night? What pain had his, Salvator's, presence at her house caused her now? He thought of Nino. Uncle Nino. Salvator realized, as if by epiphany, that he hadn't talked to Nino since he'd stopped working at the shop. All this time obsessing over Anna, and Salvator had let go of the people closest to him. Had this happened to other men? Falling in love

✝

with a woman, and in the falling ignoring all the people who, for the man's entire life, had supported and nurtured him, indeed made him the man he was?

And why, now that he thought about it, did he fall so thoroughly for this young girl? So unforeseen were these feelings for Anna! So blinding! So overwhelming! And how did he know it was love prompting him to act in these odd ways? "Oh," Rose had said once, closing her eyes and seemingly remembering her own first recognition of love, "you'll know." How did he know it wasn't infatuation? Or, worse, obsession? How did he know? How did he know anything? *Did* he know anything? He had a moment of clarity. Thought: your mother has been right all along; you don't know anything!

What do I know? I know that I miss my parents. I know that I am sitting on this couch. I know that I am confused. I know that I am a good butcher. I know that I feel something for Anna. What that something is, I don't know.

Salvator leaned over and picked up his telephone. He dialed Paulo's number.

An unfamiliar voice, feminine: "Hello."

"Is Paulo there?"

"He's out of town. Won't be back for a couple of weeks. Can I take a message?"

"Where'd he go?"

"Vegas," the woman said. "Who's this?"

"Salvator. Who're you?"

"I'm just watching his place while he's gone. Do you want to leave a message or not?"

"Just tell him I called."

"What's your name again?"

He tried calling Nino, but the number was disconnected.

Salvator slumped back on the couch and ran his fingers through his hair. He took a deep breath and decided to drop in on Nino. See what he was up to.

It was only eight-fifteen in the morning when he pulled up in front of the wreckage. Already the crews were working. Had it been so long since he'd driven by the shop that he didn't even know they'd already demolished half the block? He looked at the rubble in disbelief. A car behind him honked. He parked in the small lot across the street from his father's shop. The half of the block that used to house Polaski's Hardware lay in a pile of twisted rubble. It was as if the giant from Jack and the Beanstalk had stepped out of the clouds and squished the buildings. The demolition crews, with their huge cranes and wrecking balls and bulldozers and dumptrucks, were only three buildings away from the corner now, three buildings away from Cavriaghi's Meats.

Salvator got out of his car and sat on the bus bench facing the destruction. He looked ragged. He'd come home from the fiasco at Anna's house, didn't turn on any lights, and crashed on his bed. He was still wearing the same white-collared shirt and blue trousers, now wrinkled. He felt tired. Had everything come to this? Had his quitting and moving out precipitated the demolition of his parents' lives? Of Nino's life? Of Paulo's life? Of Anna's? A gray film of clouds hung low in the sky. Down Telegraph, towards Berkeley, the avenue looked still, motionless. A lone car, at the limits of his vision, lights on, coming toward him. He turned in his seat. He could see in to the shop from where he sat. The cases were gone, sold most likely, to some other store on a safe block. The store looked hollow. The only thing that remained of Claudio's was the painted wooden sign above the awning: big bright red letters on a green background, trimmed in white: "Cavriaghi's Meats."

He sat there for hours, squinting at the sun's disc trying to burn through the clouds towards the east, waving buses on as they slowed, watching as the crews across the street swung their wrecking ball into his father's shop. Unbelievable racket. A din compounded by the bruises on

✝

his face and in his heart. He watched as a huge tractor, its steel bucket extended liked a crooked pterodactyl wing, reached up and brought down the sign, splintering it. Did these men not care? Did they not know what they were doing? He wanted to run across the street and scream at them, tell them to stop. Stop! But he only pictured himself doing it. He only pictured himself doing it while he sat there not doing it, while he sat there not doing any damn thing but feeling sorry for himself.

By the time Salvator stood and left, he'd been sitting on the bench for six hours. His back was sore now, too. These are the kinds of feelings, he thought, that put wrinkles in your face. Everything across the street was now rubble, and the crews working over there, well, they were just working. Mopping up the detritus.

It wasn't until he got home that he thought about Nino again, realized that heaped in that mound of rubble was Nino's apartment. So where was Nino? Why hadn't he called?

He collapsed onto his couch, his mind bogged down. He tried to will himself to sleep, failed, went to his knife drawer and removed his sharpening stone, steel, and the first knife he saw: the boning knife. The knife was sharp enough, but he thought perhaps running a blade along the whet stone might get his mind off things. It didn't. With each push and pull of the knife, a new thought wandered into consciousness. Push: stab Toscana. Pull: miss my parents. Push: go see Anna. Pull: forget about Anna. Push: Push: Push: Pull: Pull: Pull. Ah, to hell with it, he said aloud, and dropped the knife on the counter without steeling it.

He went back to the couch, deliberated for a moment, then called his parents. He wanted to cry—but didn't: couldn't?—as he told his mother what he saw on the avenue, how sorry he was that he'd left, that he'd never meant to hurt them. She listened and cried for him, told him that she missed her son, that she really missed her son. Then, after they'd both calmed down, worked through some of the memories, Rose said, "I have to tell you something, Salvator."

"What is it?" Salvator said.

"Anna's here, at our house."

Salvator did not know what to say.

Rose continued. "She got here really early this morning. She says she's run away, that her father beats her."

"That's true, mom. He beat me up last night. How'd she get there?"

Her voice rose an octave: "He beat you up last night?"

"I'm okay. Really. I was supposed to meet Anna during the basketball game, but her friend Lisa—"

"Lisa's the one who brought her up here. They're both here."

Salvator shook his head. Wondered, how'd they pull that off?

"Did you call the police?" Rose said.

"No," Salvator said. "I wasn't even supposed to be there. He has a restraining order against me."

"A restraining order? What'd you do?"

"I sang songs to his daughter and sent her flowers," he said. "I guess he didn't like that." He paused. "Is she okay? Can I talk to her?"

"They're sleeping right now. What's this restraining order thing?"

"Don't worry about it, it's nothing. Where's Dad? Does he know she's there?"

"He's the one that let her in, Salvator. He didn't recognize her at first. She was wearing sunglasses and a baseball cap. He let her in when she told him why she'd run away."

"Has she called her parents?" Salvator said.

"No," Rose said. "She doesn't want to. She doesn't want to go back."

"If they find out she's there, Mom, you guys are in big trouble."

"I know," she said. "Dad and I talked about it last night and decided we'll call her parents tomorrow if she doesn't. But we want to give her a chance to rest. She's very scared."

"I'm coming up," Salvator said.

"I think that's a good idea, Salvator," she said. "She said she didn't want you to know, but I think it might do her good to see you. Poor girl. She really does like you, from all she said."

"How'd she find you guys?"

"She said you'd told her where we'd moved, so she just drove up here and looked us up. She didn't want to go to any of her friends' houses because she knew those would be the first places her parents looked. They don't know we've moved. She thought she'd be safe up here."

"And Dad's okay with this? And you?"

"What are we going to do, Salvator? Tell this girl to go away? We can't turn her out when she's this far from home. At least right now she's safe."

"I'm coming up. I'm leaving right now."

"No, don't leave now," Rose said. "You wouldn't get here till after midnight. You're better off sleeping and leaving in the morning."

He hung up the phone, excited and a little scared. Her parents must be scared to death right now, not knowing where she is. Maybe this'll wake that Toscana up. Rose sounded good, actually. But his father? Well, he couldn't be against Anna's staying at his house if she was there. His parents. Good people, those two. Salvator put a pair of underwear, clean socks, a clean T-shirt, and his toothbrush in a plastic grocery bag, and left.

FIFTEEN

Thick traffic out of Oakland. Even now, at 6:30 in the evening, nearly an hour past "rush hour"—they should call it "rush three hours" in the San Francisco Bay Area—I-580 was choked with cars. He'd smacked the steering wheel with the palm of his scarred hand when he saw the backed up lines of cars. Why would all these people want to drive so much? Work in San Francisco, live in Santa Rosa. Work in San Francisco, live in Petaluma. Or Sebastopol. Some people even commuted to the City by the Bay from Cloverdale, a miniature town nearly sixty miles north of the City. How did they do it? Nearly every car Salvator looked into: one person. And every one of those people had their lives and families. Were any of them on their way to see their love? Maybe the man coming up behind him, eighty or ninety miles per hour, maybe that man just had a call. "Mr. Smith, your wife's delivering." Or maybe he's on a getaway mission, having just robbed a bank. The elderly couple, over there, to the right, whipping along at all of forty-miles per hour. Was it possible they drove slowly on purpose? Were they distracted by something?

He crossed the Richmond Bridge, stayed in the left lane, then pulled up on to Highway 101, that great smooth highway that twisted through some of the most beautiful terrain in the world. Unlike its cousin, the I-5, which split through the central valley of the state in one long, monotonous

129

†

straight line, Highway 101 curved and dipped along the western edge of California's Coastal Ranges, running, at some points, along waterways like the Russian River and, further north, the Eel River.

The traffic didn't ease up until Salvator passed Santa Rosa, the last big city before Eureka and Arcata. Four more hours to go. At least. He was in wine country. The sun, down and out of sight to his left, still gave off enough dusky light that Salvator could make out the shapes of the hills, see the darkened rows of grape vines, tangled Lilliputian men and women, arms stretched out to their sides, heads arced to the sky.

Now it was dark, and he could see behind him only a few cars, other lonely people on their way north. He passed through Sonoma County and into Mendocino County. He liked it here in these sparsely populated Northern counties. Once, when he and his parents were driving up to camp in Big Lagoon, he had had a feeling of pity for the people of these small Northern towns. He couldn't have been more than nine or ten at the time, but now, as he drove this road, he remembered how sorry he felt for them that they had to drive so far to get to McDonald's. His perspective now was different, though, and he suspected it fell more in line with the true sentiments of those small towners: McDonald's couldn't be far enough away. Nor could the malls and smog and noise and clutter of the city. Indeed, now that he reflected upon it, he thought that the people living in these remote nooks of California's hills and mountains, yes, these people knew more about living than he did. They knew peace and quiet. Peace in its genuine sense. Not peace for a minute a day, not meditation in the middle of a ruckus. But genuine, soothing calmness. What was the word? He tapped his forefinger on the dashboard. Solace. That's it. He wondered how many of Northern California's inhabitants had fled the bigger cities for the tranquillity of a stream, for dirt that's not transplanted from a bag, for trees that have stood for decades, or, in some places, millennia.

He was passing Ukiah now, his thoughts winding along with the turns in the road. A mile past Ukiah he realized he needed gas, and, twenty minutes later, Salvator stopped in Willits, a small town about two and a half hours north of Oakland. He filled the car with fuel and got a microwaved burrito and a cup of coffee to go at the gas station. He ate and drank as he drove.

He stopped again in Laytonville, twenty minutes later, to take a leak and buy another cup of coffee.

Richardson Grove. The beginning of the Redwood Curtain. How beautiful were these trees? Some of them seemed as big around as his bedroom. Even during daylight, this dense grove of ancient redwoods looked dark. If he'd had time, Salvator would have gotten out and walked down to the Eel River, listened to it. But he didn't have time. He needed to get home.

Home? The thought surprised him, like the unexpected flash of a camera in a dark room. He just called his parents' new house *home*, and he'd never even seen it; he'd never even been invited! But that was it. Home is not the house. Like his mother had said, it's the people in the house.

He passed Garberville, the small town with the best hamburgers in the universe. Every summer that they traveled they would stop in at the burger joint there on Garberville's main street—he couldn't remember the name of it now—and sit and eat the big, juicy, fat-dripping burgers. His dad would weave stories as they ate, tall tales about Bigfoot and the ghosts of gold miners. Oh, how he wanted one of those glorious burgers now. To be nine again, and under the spell of his father's voice.

The air had cooled considerably. Now, everywhere his headlights beamed, trees and trees and more trees. Not at all like the concrete and glass of Oakland. Not at all. No bullet holes here. No trash in the gutters because there were no gutters. No noise. No shouting customers. No buildings scraping the sky, mucking up a perfectly good horizon.

Salvator rubbed his eyes and stretched his neck to each side, then forward and backward. An odd sensation now, a sloughing off. Of what? He felt lighter, as if for years he'd been tethered to the ground, trying to float away, and now the cord had been cut. And what was this? He pictured himself now streaming in to the future, his history streaking behind him like the long tail of a comet: his birth the distant tip of the tail, that farthest,

†

unreachable memory, everything thickening, growing more and more dense, molecules upon molecules bunching up like metallic particles scattered towards a magnet, until everything, the entire weight of every single thing he'd ever done coalesced in his head, the mass of the comet itself punching a hole through time and space.

Through Eureka now, the largest Californian city on the 101 north of Ukiah. Highway 101 runs right through the center of Eureka, past Pierson Building Supply, home of the world's largest hammer, past assorted fast food restaurants, past small town diners. Much of Eureka's main street was lined with closed down businesses. Salvator remembered Telegraph Avenue. The same here: boarded up store fronts, vacant buildings, "for lease" signs. He'd heard in a news report a few weeks earlier that Eureka's crime rate had risen dramatically over the last ten years, something to do with drugs. Sad thing, really, Salvator thought, that people leave big cities to move to small cities like Eureka, but forget, in their moving, that they bring their big city problems with them.

He passed by Arcata, wound up and over the mound of highway near McKinleyville, then back up and into Trinidad. He turned right at the end of the off ramp, climbing a steep and narrow two lane road to the east of Highway 101. After a few more right and left turns, Salvator leaned forward in his seat, squinting, trying to make out the landmark his mother had said to look for: a white mail box on a huge-linked and welded chain. Number 247, Sandalwood Road. He turned into the dirt driveway, made his way up to the house, and finally shut off the car at twelve-twenty-seven in the morning.

The house was much smaller than their house in Oakland, and, he had to be honest, much more beautiful. The driveway ended to the right of the front door. On either side of the front door, which was lit by a dim yellow light, were two sash windows trimmed in white paint. The siding of the house, he realized, was not painted at all: old gray wooden shingles, weathered by the salty ocean air. Salvator grabbed the plastic bag from the passenger's seat and stepped out of the car. He could immediately smell

✝

the ocean. He took in a deep breath and closed his eyes. It was much cooler here than in Oakland. A truck shifted gears in the distance. A breeze picked up and swayed the trees surrounding the house, a faint rustling of millions of needles. Could he hear the ocean? He cocked his head forward. Tried. Thought for a moment that he did, but he couldn't be sure. He walked down the driveway a little and tried again.

"Nice up here, eh?" Claudio said.

Salvator spun around, startled.

"She's in there," Claudio said, pointing over his shoulder with his thumb. He walked up to where Salvator was standing and folded his arms over his chest.

Claudio looked Salvator up and down, grunted, then snorted, then jerked his head in the direction of the house. "Aren't you going to say anything?" Claudio said.

"Is she okay?" Salvator said, carving a line in the dirt with the toe of his right shoe. He didn't have the guts to look Claudio in the face. He suddenly felt very, very sad.

"They're all sleeping," Claudio said.

"Does she know I'm coming?" He must be mad at me, Salvator thought. He must be.

"We didn't tell her."

Then his mouth said it without first consulting with his brain: "I'm sorry, Dad," Salvator said.

Claudio shook his head. "You don't need to be sorry," Claudio said. Again, he wagged his head in the direction of the house. "We'll talk." Claudio patted Salvator a few times on the back. "Come on."

"Shouldn't we call her parents?" Salvator said.

"We'll do that in the morning. We'll tell them she got here tonight and that you were already up here." Claudio looked at Salvator's face under the yellow bug light. He grabbed Salvator's chin with his right hand. "That bastard really smacked you, didn't he?"

"Yeah," Salvator said. "He got me pretty good."

"I could kill him."

"Kill him for Anna," Salvator said. "I can protect myself."

"Doesn't look like you did a very good job protecting yourself, Salvator."

"I wasn't going to hit him back when he had that much anger on his side. I'm not as dumb as you look."

Claudio smiled and opened the door. "Let's go in before we freeze to death."

"So you like the new house?"

"Love it. Can't hear anything but the ocean in the distance, the wind in the trees, and your heart in your chest out here"—Oh brother, Salvator thought—"Best thing your mother and I ever did, Sal."

Salvator raised his eyebrows, slightly. Rare thing for Claudio to call him Sal. That was usually reserved for the most tender of moments, like the times Claudio reminisced about his own father. "I couldn't hear the ocean," Salvator said. "That's what I was trying to do out there."

"Takes a couple of days. You have to adjust to the quiet."

Even Morris Montgomery's apartment isn't this quiet, Salvator thought. All a matter of perspective. The house wasn't as big inside as the Oakland house, though it had the illusion of being bigger because the rooms—at least the rooms he now saw—were spacious and wide open. The kitchen was to the left, and they'd entered into what must have been the living room. To the right was the dining room. No walls separated these three main rooms, which was what gave the house its bigger-than-it-really-is feeling. A log burned in the huge, old black-iron woodstove against the wall in the living room. Beside the stove, a pile of wood the same color as the siding on the house, the ends of the logs cracked like the palms of Claudio's hands. To the right and left of the stove were two doors: the bedrooms.

Claudio pointed to the one on the right. He said in a half-whisper, "They're in there."

"Lisa's still here?" Salvator said. Now that he thought about it, he hadn't seen any other cars when he drove up.

Claudio nodded. "She called her parents when they got here, told them what was going on. Mom talked to her mom, and they agreed that it'd be a good idea for Lisa to stay with Anna, at least for a couple of days. Good parents."

"Good friends," Salvator said.

Claudio nodded and turned towards the kitchen. Over his shoulder, Claudio said: "The other room's mine and your mom's. You can sleep out here on the couch."

Salvator set his bag down on the couch. The *new* couch. A couch he'd never seen before: mahogany arms and legs, a plush, thickly padded seat and back the color of—what was that color his mother loved?—malachite? The couch could easily fit four adults. It acted as the barrier between the living and the dining room beyond. There, in the dining room, was the old table he'd grown up with, its familiar dark gloss. When he was seven he'd crawled under the table and scribbled his full name— Salvator Claudio Cavriaghi—and the date in purple crayon on the table's unfinished underside. Had his parent's discovered this while moving?

He walked over to the counter that separated the kitchen from the living room and leaned over, stretching his arms out across the avocado-green tile counter top and dipping his head in between his arms, easing the tension in his back. He made a few circles with his head, then, in a larger sweep, with his hands on his hips, he hunched forward and swung his entire torso in two slow moving ellipses. "Geez, I'm out of shape," he said, more to himself than to Claudio.

"Are you hungry?" Claudio said. Claudio looked tired. Happy, but tired. His hair was slicked back, and his belly stuck out, slightly. He'd never had much of gut. Nothing like Nino in his hey day. Claudio reached up into the cupboard above the sink. "There's some salami and cheese in the fridge. Why don't you make yourself a sandwich?"

"I'm not hungry," Salvator said.

Claudio waved it off. "Come and eat some food so I can go to bed." He stepped over to the refrigerator and took out the salami and cheese and a loaf of bread and made a couple of sandwiches. He pointed to the small white table against the wall in the kitchen. Salvator sat down. "I'll have one with you," Claudio said. He put some water on to boil and made hot chocolate.

"You know, son," Claudio said as he brought Salvator his sandwich and cocoa, "I still don't like this idea of you and a seventeen year old girl. She's a *girl*, Salvator, a *girl*." He went back to the counter to get his food and drink and returned to the table.

Salvator chewed down a bite of the sandwich. Few things in the world as satisfying as a plain salami-on-sourdough after midnight. Of course, this one was going to cost him.

"You're a grown man," Claudio said. He shook his head.

Salvator checked his anger, held his breath a moment longer than usual.

"You were five or six years old before she was even a thought."

"I love her, Dad, and I won't apologize for it." Salvator wiped his face with a napkin, took a sip of the cocoa, wiped his face again. "Besides, who are you to talk? You're just as much older than Mom."

"What do you know about love? What makes you think you know anything about love?"

Salvator fiddled with his sandwich, took another bite. Thought: Haven't even been here ten minutes. Said: "I see you and Mom, and I think, 'Those two people love each other.' That's how I know about love. I watch people."

Claudio rolled his eyes. "Big deal," he said.

Salvator continued. "Remember in the hospital, when I cut my hand, how her father looked? There's no love there. No *real* love. You could just tell by the way he handled her. Tell by the way Toscana shook Anna. No love in that house. I know it"—he patted his chest—"and I feel it."

"There's a lot of different kinds of love, Salvator, not all of it healthy."

"You think it's unhealthy for me to love Anna?"

"I think you go overboard."

✝

"Overboard?" His voice was a little louder than he'd hoped. "What's that mean?"

Claudio waved his hand in the air. "All the singing, the carrying on. That's overboard. You love her? Say it once, and be done with it."

"You know what, Dad? This world needs a lot more singing and carrying on. That's what this world needs. More singing Salvators."

Claudio sat back in his chair and rolled his eyes again. He started to say something, then just flicked his hand in the air.

"I'm serious," Salvator said. "I'm trying to *win* her love, *earn* it. You should do a little more earning of Mom's love. You have any idea—"

Claudio leaned forward, thrust his right forefinger at Salvator: "Don't tell me how to love my wife."

"She may be your wife, but she's my mother," Salvator said, keeping his voice low, trying not to wake anyone else up. "You're pissed off at me because I finally did something for myself." Salvator, with exaggerated drama, looked around the house. "Doesn't look to me like you've got too much to complain about."

Claudio rubbed his eyes.

"Look," Salvator said, "I didn't come up here to fight with you. There's a lot of unhappy people in this world, and she was one of them until I started singing to her and sending her flowers and writing her poems."

Claudio said, "You wrote her poems?" He shook his head and rolled his eyes again.

But this time Salvator thought he saw the twitch of a smile on his father's face. Deep lines in that face, Salvator thought.

They sat and talked for another half hour, Claudio relenting a bit and finally admitting that Salvator must have *something* going for him—he smiled here—since Anna does seem like a genuinely nice girl. "Very polite," Claudio had said, "and fragile."

Salvator untucked his shirt, took off his socks, folded the pillow on the couch in half, and pulled a thin blanket over his mid-section. It was quite warm in the room even though the fire in the woodstove had died down.

"Need anything else before I turn this off?" Claudio said, pointing at the light switch.

Salvator shook his head.

Claudio switched off the light. The curtains on the windows were open and some residual moonlight filled the room with a fuzzy, dim light. Claudio walked over to Salvator and bent down and kissed him on the forehead.

"Good night, Sal," Claudio said.

Salvator reached up and rubbed Claudio's forearm. "Good night."

~~~

The sounds and smells of breakfast woke Salvator from sleep. Before he opened his eyes he identified the food: bacon crackling in the huge cast iron skillet, eggs-over-medium frying up on the griddle, toast burning in the toaster—who knows why, but his father loved burnt toast—the swish of a wooden spoon stirring up some orange juice, his mother lightly tapping the spoon on the rim of the carafe. He heard the sink fill with water, his mother whisper something, his father answer back in whisper. He could not make out what they'd said to each other.

A few years ago when he'd gone to visit Paulo at one of Paulo's training sessions—Paulo had tried a few times to get Salvator to start practicing ninjutsu, always to no avail—Paulo took a few minutes to explain an exercise he and his friends were working on. Paulo's training group consisted of their sensei, or teacher, Stephen J. Malmstrom, and six men and five women. On the day Salvator came to visit, ten of the students and their sensei were standing in a circle facing one of the male students, who stood in the center of the circle, blindfolded. The exercise went like this: of the eleven people standing in the circle, ten of them had to send positive emotions to the person in the center and one of them had to send murderous intentions towards the practitioner in the middle. The person in the middle had to point to the person sending the hateful emotions.

Paulo later explained that what they were working on was both the perception of emotions in other people and the development of emotions in the self. Whoever stood in the center of the circle was trying to sense emotions coming towards him; whoever stood in the circumference of the circle was working on sending specific emotions out of her body. They had let Salvator try a few times, and, though he failed at the exercise then, he had worked on developing his intuition regarding other people's emotions. He'd gotten fairly good at sensing the emotional state of customers as they came into the store, and now, as he stretched and yawned on the couch, he felt an overwhelming sense of happiness radiating from his parents. Particularly his mother.

He got up and walked over to the kitchen counter.

"You look terrible," Rose said.

Salvator said, "You should talk."

"That's how you greet your mother when she's cooking you breakfast?" She was smiling.

"What the heck did you do to your hair?" Salvator said.

"I dyed it black," she said, flicking a flirtatious look over her shoulder towards Claudio, who, Salvator could have sworn, had raised his eyebrows up and down a few times, as if propositioning her.

"Oh Jesus," Salvator said. "Cut this out. I don't need to see this kind of thing first thing in the morning."

Rose smiled and walked over to her husband and hugged him around the neck. They kissed, and, for the first time in a very long time, Salvator thought his parents were in love.

"See these sunflowers?" Rose said, pointing to the vase on the table. "Your father picked those for me this morning from the field behind the house."

Salvator pulled his head back, shocked. He pointed to Claudio and said to Rose: "This guy did that?" His father did something romantic? Did *anything* for Rose?

Rose hugged her son again.

✝

"Don't make him feel wanted, Rose," Claudio said. "We don't want him to think he's welcome here."

They really are happy, Salvator thought. How long had it been since they'd both given him crap at the same time? Five, six years? More?

"Seems like things are going pretty well for you two," Salvator said.

"Selling that store was the best thing that your father ever did for me," Rose said.

"*For* you?" Salvator said.

Claudio was smiling at Rose.

"Salvator," she said, "I had to beg him to get rid of that thing."

"You two don't tell me anything," Salvator said. He went over to the stove and got himself some breakfast then returned to the table.

"Why should we?" Claudio said.

"I'm your son."

"Big deal," Claudio said. "You're my son. The same one who walked out a few months ago, remember?"

"Looks to me like that worked out well for all of us," Salvator said.

"Indeed it did," Claudio said. Claudio took a bite of toast then got up and took his plate to the sink. Then he told Rose to sit down and he served her breakfast.

Rose leaned over to Salvator and whispered, "He even does the dishes now."

Salvator looked at his father. Was that even the same man? He looked like the same man, the one who usually kept his recliner anchored to the ground by the sheer weight of his body. The same one who expected things done for him. "What happened?" Salvator said to Rose. "Are you slipping something into his meatballs?"

Rose smiled. "No," she said. "Ever since we moved up here, he's been like this."

"What's wrong, Sal?" Claudio said. "You didn't think I had it in me?"

Salvator shrugged. "I haven't seen you two look this happy since I can't remember when."

✝

"I tell you, son," Claudio said, "when you get to be my age, you start thinking about things. Things that people your age don't think about."

"Like what?" Salvator said.

"Like the fact that you've lived more years than you've got left to live. Some people begin to realize things early in their lives. Some people begin to realize things late. I'm the late kind. It took me all these years to realize I'd been driving your mother crazy. But she's so damn good she never said anything until this offer of the money for the store came through."

Rose cut in: "I told him I loved him but that he never showed me he loved me."

"And I said," Claudio continued, "'what about all those years going to work so you didn't have to?' And it took me a while, Sal, but she finally showed me that bringing home a paycheck to a woman is not what constitutes love. I could bring home a million dollars, and that doesn't count like doing the dishes does. Or going out and picking her some flowers."

"Nino had a little to do with it, though," Rose said.

Nino, Salvator thought. How he'd changed! Giving love advice to other men!

"Well," Claudio said. "He was the one convinced me I was being a jackass."

Claudio started washing the dishes and speaking over his shoulder. "You know, Salvator, that girl in there"—he wagged his head in the direction of the room Anna was sleeping in—"she's a nice girl. She's very young, though."

"What he's trying to say, Salvator," Rose said, "is that he gives you his blessing."

"His blessing?" Salvator said. "He was giving me a hard time about it just last night!" Salvator buttered up a slice of toast and ate it. "He was telling me she's too young and all this other stuff."

"We've been talking about it a lot," Rose said. "Your father finally understands—"

"I finally understand that you're your own man, Salvator. And you've got to do what you think is right. And it doesn't matter what I think anymore. You have to make your own mistakes and learn from them, as I did."

At that, Anna and Lisa emerged from the bedroom. Salvator stood, looking at her expectantly. She smiled at him, as did Lisa.

"Go hug her, you idiot," Claudio said.

Anna was wearing a T-shirt and sweat pants and had a faint black and blue mark around her right eye. She looked pale, as if she'd been running a fever for a few days. Her hair was brushed out and pulled back in pony tail. How beautiful she looks even now, Salvator thought. Suddenly he felt very said, wounded. Anna's face looked deeply tired, distraught even, as though she'd been through a horrible war, had witnessed atrocities.

"I guess they called you," she said.

Salvator nodded. He hugged her, and he felt, finally, the tender curve of her shoulders, the nudge of her chin at his neck. She hugged him back, tightly, their skin smooth and warm together, as if they'd spent the night under the same covers. He felt now a sense of groundedness, as if in hugging Anna he'd finally reached a great plateau, one he'd been hiking towards all his life.

"Would you like some breakfast, you two?" Rose asked the girls.

"Sure," Lisa said. Lisa rubbed Anna's back and walked into the kitchen.

First time we're this close, Salvator thought, and my breath could kill a small dog. He shook his head at the thought. A vision of Toscana swinging his fat arms. A memory of how hard his heart beat in his chest as he ran from Toscana. "I'm sorry he hits you," Salvator said.

"Not your fault," Anna said. She looked away from Salvator. "It's been going on forever," she said. "He'll never stop."

Anna and Salvator sat down on the couch. Claudio brought Anna a glass of orange juice. "Thank you," she said, taking the glass in her frail hands.

"So what are we going to do?" Salvator said.

"We?" she said.

"Yeah, we."

†

She smiled, then, more serious: "I don't want to go back, Salvator. He's gotten worse. He won't let me out of his sight."

"Anna?" Lisa said. "You should have some breakfast. It's really good."

"How'd you get out of the house?" Salvator said.

"Just left, that's all. Waited till they were asleep and left." She relaxed into the couch. She kept her eyes on Salvator, though, trying, he could see, to exude strength. Which, to a degree, she was accomplishing. He could see behind the gaze though the fragile ego, how embarrassed she felt, ashamed.

"What about your mother?" Salvator asked.

"She acts like she doesn't know what's going on, but he hits her just as much as he hits me."

"Why doesn't she leave him?"

"It's not easy for a woman like my mother to leave her fancy house and car and lifestyle. She's got an image to maintain, the powerful lawyer, you know." Anna waved her hands in the air. "She just keeps popping her pills and pretending that life's just fine."

Salvator wanted to reach out and put his hand on her knee, but he didn't. He wanted to wrap his arms around her again and feel her breath through his chest. But he didn't. He said: "So what are we going to do, Anna? You have to go home. You're not eighteen yet."

"But I'll be eighteen in three months," she said, pushing a straggling strand of hair back over her ear, "and as soon as I graduate from high-school, I'm moving out."

"But what about now?"

"Lisa and I were talking about it with your mom yesterday, and we all agree I shouldn't go back unless they agree to family counseling."

"What if they don't agree? I mean, your father's going to be furious."

"If they don't agree, then I'll petition the court to go live with my grandmother in San Leandro until I finish high-school."

"And what if the court doesn't let you do that?"

"Then I'll just run away and stay away and there's nothing they can do about that once I'm eighteen."

✝

"It's not that easy, Anna."

"Anything's easier than living in that house."

Salvator thought about his life, how, compared to Anna's, he had nothing to complain about. He remembered once, when he was griping about how he never got to travel, his father had told him about an old tradition—was it a Jewish tradition? he couldn't remember—that had people write their problems down on a piece of paper. Then people would gather around a tree and pin their problems to the tree. The idea was that by walking around the tree and reading the problem's of other people, you began to realize you didn't have any problems, that everything was relative, and that you'd never want some else's problems because they invariably seemed worse than your own. Surely, in this instance, what Salvator considered painful—a cut on his hand, dropping a piece of meat, never going to college—these things did not compare in the least to what Anna had endured. At seventeen, sitting there beside him, her young eyes already looked wise.

"She's a good friend," Salvator said, poking his head in Lisa's direction.

Anna nodded. "Best in the world."

"Come eat," Rose said.

Salvator leaned over a little closer to Anna. "You better eat something or you'll ruin her whole day."

Anna smiled and nodded, whispered, "When we got here, she put out enough food to feed half of Oakland."

Salvator and Anna stood and went into the kitchen. Anna sat down between Rose and Lisa, and Salvator went over to the counter top and poured himself a cup of coffee. As the women talked, Claudio said to Salvator, "You know, son, she really likes you. She's thinks you're a pretty big deal."

Salvator stuck out his lower lip and bobbed his head up and down. "What do *you* think about me?" he said to his father.

Claudio paused and scratched the back of his neck. "You're alright," he said, putting his arm around Salvator's shoulders.

✝

Salvator laughed and elbowed Claudio in the stomach. "You're an old fart." Salvator thought a moment, then said to Anna and Lisa, "Hey, when you two are done eating, we should go down to the beach."

"You two go ahead and go," Lisa said, "I've got to call my mother."

Within the hour, Salvator had showered and changed. Anna emerged from the bathroom wearing the same sweat pants she'd had on at breakfast and a clean, dark green sweatshirt. She carried her shoes in her hand.

The drive to the beach took only a few minutes. "I feel weird," he'd said on the way there. "I don't know what to say to you." "Say it when we get to the sand," she'd said. They parked the car in the first turnout they came to, sat there for a moment in silence watching the thick fog roll along the shore, then got out and took the narrow, rocky trail down to the beach. She did this barefoot, which Salvator found remarkable since his feet were soft as a baby's.

"Take your shoes off," Anna said when they got down from the trail and onto the beach.

He did this, not wanting to let on that he'd never done it before.

"Haven't you ever been barefoot on a beach?" she said.

He looked away and laughed a little. "No," he said. He tried to change the subject. "That's Wedding Rock over there," he said, pointing towards the north at a huge mass of mussel-coated stone poking out of the water.

"Is that a hint?" Anna said. She'd stepped ahead of him a pace or two.

"No," Salvator said, smiling. Oh yes, even with all she's been through she carries herself like a noble woman. "That's not a hint, that's a fact." Okay, so maybe it was a hint. Big deal. She seemed nearly to float out here near the ocean; indeed, for a moment, he thought perhaps she hadn't left any footprints in the damp sand.

They walked nearly a mile up the beach before turning around, their conversation covering everything from the first time he'd seen her in the shop through the last time he'd seen her at the basketball game. He picked up a few rocks along the way and flung them into the ocean. She confessed that she'd found him "cute" when she first saw him in Cavriaghi's

Meats, that she'd never be able to get the image of that "big piece of meat" sailing out of his hands out of her mind.

He bent down and picked up a whole sand dollar and gave it to her. "You know," he said, "if you break that open you'll find birds."

She cocked her head back, curious.

"Really," he said. He saw another sand dollar a few feet away, picked it up, then snapped it in two. Three miniature shells tumbled from the broken dollar, each one shaped like a swan in flight. He placed the fragile creatures into her palm then folded her fingers over them. "I've always believed," he said, "that if you think hard enough and give your sadness to the birds, they will carry the sadness away for you." He was still holding her outstretched hand. "Close your eyes," he said. "Now think of things that you don't want anymore and give those things to the birds." He paused a moment as she did what he asked. She tilted her head back, then forward, thinking. She opened her eyes. "Okay, good," he said. "Come on," he said, and led her by the hand to the edge of the surf. "Now throw the birds to the ocean and they will carry whatever you gave them away."

She said nothing to him. She took in a deep breath then, her arm arcing, she tossed the birds into the Pacific. She trusts me, he thought. He said, "This is the Pacific Ocean, Anna. Pacific means to make peace."

She cocked her head again, and the look on her face was a mix between, "You're crazy" and "Thank you."

Salvator pointed to a huge piece of bleached driftwood about fifty yards down the beach and said, "Let's go sit down."

"Salvator," Anna said as they sat down, "why do you like me so much? I mean, you're about the only guy in the world whose ever paid me any attention and, well, we pretty much don't even know each other."

"What's there to know except that we are together, right now, on this beach? To me, that says everything." He crossed his legs and turned to face her. She watched him closely. "Look, Anna," he said, "ever since I can remember, a woman with long black hair and green eyes pops up in my dreams. For the longest time I didn't understand why this woman kept appearing in my dreams. Then one day, I don't know, maybe four or five years ago, I was cutting meat and it came to me in a burst of awareness: this was the woman I was going to marry. I swear to God. I know it sounds crazy, but that's the truth. I knew as soon as I thought it that it was true. I knew without a doubt that whoever she was, I'd meet her and we'd get married."

Anna looked down at the sand and drew a circle with her finger. Beyond them, soft waves rolled up onto shore, foamed, then retreated. The sound of the waves lulled Salvator into calmness. He reached over and touched her chin. "Anna, I swear to you it's true. There've been a few women who've come in to the shop with long black hair and green eyes and not one of them stands out in my memory. I didn't feel a thing when they came in. But, Anna," he paused and took in a deep breath, "I knew from the second I saw you that you were the woman in my dreams and that I had to do everything I possibly could to win you over."

"Why didn't you tell me this before?"

"I don't know," he said. "Probably because I was supposed to tell you now." He leaned forward and took her hands in his. The strong scent of the salt air calmed him. "Anna, I believe everything happens for a reason. I don't believe in coincidences. I believe you came into the shop that day because I needed you as much as you needed me, as much as our parents needed this to happen. Look at how much has changed in these past months! You're out of that house. You might still be there if you didn't have this crazy Sicilian singing to you!" He paused, then: "If I had told you this sooner you'd have written me off as a nut."

"You are a little nutty," she said, smiling.

"Absolutely!" he said. Many times during their walk Salvator had considered kissing her, and he did that now, leaning further forward, bringing his lips to hers. They both relaxed into the kiss, as if they'd finally come in to peaceful waters. As he pulled away, he said, "I love you, Anna. And I can't help it. I simply love you."

✝

She started to cry and he pulled her to him, turned her around so she could lean back into his chest. He crossed his arms over her, and she crossed her arms over him. "Oh Salvator," she said, "I've always told myself that when the right guy comes along, I'll know it. I know it's cliche, I know it's what everybody says, but I always really believed it was true. My father, he doesn't like your father. He thinks your dad is 'lower-class.' He thinks you're 'below' me. But I've never felt that way, Salvator. I've always felt connected to you from the first time I saw you. My God! It was so cute when you dropped that meat. I knew I'd caused it. Oh, that felt really good!" She was smiling now. She turned around and faced him. "That felt really, really good." She ran a hand down his left arm, tilted her head, and said, "I guess I love you, too."

"You guess?" he said.

"I mean, I do, really, I do. I mean I never expected to feel romantic about a guy. All the guys I've dated have been jerks."

"*All* the guys?"

"I've only kissed a few," she said, mischievous. "Seriously though. All the guys in high school want is sex. That's it. They lie to each other about who they've slept with. They lure girls in with false promises, sleep with them, then throw them away. And you never once gave me that impression. You never made me feel like an object. I'd get shivers when you sang to me."

"Shivers? Really? That's good," he lifted his eyebrows up and down a few times. Then, rubbing his hands together, Salvator said in a mock evil-scientist voice, "So, my plan is working."

She nodded. "Oh, it's working alright." She leaned over and kissed him, leaned back, and cupped his face in her hands. "It's definitely working."

As they walked back to the car, Anna said she wanted to go to college and study biology, maybe go into teaching.

"I hear that Humboldt State up here is a good school," Salvator said. "Maybe you could apply there?"

"What are you trying to say?"

"I'm trying to say I want us to be together, and I want you to move up here so we *can* be together. There's a lot we can do together, Anna," Salvator said. "I can start a shop up here while you go to school. You said you want to be a teacher? I bet there's plenty of schools around here for you to get work when you graduate."

"But what about your apartment and all your friends down in Oakland?"

"I only have my parents and Nino and Paulo. I really don't get out enough because I'm always working in the shop. Besides, from what my father tells me, the cost of living up here is a whole lot less than it is down in Oakland."

Anna nodded and smiled. Salvator hadn't felt this sense of tranquility in quite a few months.

"You know, Anna," Salvator said as they pulled out of the tiny parking lot, "ever since I first saw you I've been cutting meat in your name."

"That's gross," she said.

He smiled. "You have many steaks named in your honor."

"Say something in Italian," she said.

> *Tu sei la purità.*
> *Tu sei la vita della mia vita.*

"What does that mean?" she said.

He said:

> You are purity.
> You are the life of my life.

SIXTEEN

By two in the afternoon, Anna had reached her mother at work and explained where she was and what was going on. "I'm going to stay up here one more night," Anna said to her mother. "Lisa and I will leave early tomorrow morning. We'll be home by noon."

Salvator was sitting next to her when she hung up the telephone. He couldn't believe how anxious he felt as Anna spoke to her mother. "She must have agreed to counseling," he said.

"She did," Anna said. Anna leaned back in her chair and rubbed her forehead.

Lisa was sitting across from them at the kitchen table. "What about your dad, is he going to go? He's the one that needs it."

"She said he'd go," Anna said. "She'd convince him."

"Yeah, right," Lisa said. She waved her hand in the air. "That'll be the day."

Anna looked at Salvator. "My mother said my dad wants you arrested for stalking."

"Stalking?"

"He says everything you've been doing is stalking." Anna was shaking her head now.

"Do you feel stalked?" Salvator asked.

"No," Anna said. "Of course not."

Salvator reached over and touched Anna's arm.

"My mom said she'll try to get him to drop that idea," Anna said, "but she can't promise anything because he's completely freaked out about me leaving."

"When he finds out where you've been, he'll *really* have a shit," Lisa said.

Anna leaned over and kissed Salvator on the cheek. "Your parents have been extremely nice, Salvator. And so have you."

He smiled. "I told my dad I'd go see his shop out back. You two want to come out there with me?"

"No," they said in unison. Then Anna said, "That's boy stuff."

Salvator stood, rubbed Anna's back between her shoulder blades, kissed her on top of the head, and went out the back door of his parent's home. His mother was kneeling down in the garden, her hands thoroughly coated with fresh, black topsoil.

"So things with you and Dad are going good?" he said. She looked radiant.

"Salvator," she said, setting her trowel down, "I've never been happier. He's the Claudio I married again. He's passionate about *me* again, not that damn shop."

The scent of the fresh soil was strong to Salvator. "You still doing that meditation thing?"

"You mean yoga?" she said.

"Yeah, that's it."

"You should remember that by now, Salvator."

"Yeah," he said. "You still doing it, though?"

"Every day," she said. "And your father's started doing it with me."

"It's not right to lie to your children, Mom. Sets a bad example."

"I'm not lying. Just don't tell him I told you. That was part of the deal of him doing it. Me not telling you."

✝

Salvator laughed. "Is he back there?" Salvator pointed towards the back of the property. Through a small grove of redwoods he could see what looked like a small, cedar-shingled shack.

She nodded. "That's where he is," she said.

Salvator bent down and grabbed a handful of the new soil. "What are you planting?"

"Plants," she said.

"You're funny," he said.

"Herbs," she said. "Our neighbor down the road, Betsy, she's been showing me how to do this. These new ones should grow nice and strong if I take good care of them."

Salvator nodded and stood, released the handful of dirt from his hand. "Well, I'm sure they'll do fine, Mom." He touched her on the shoulder and headed off in the direction of the shack.

He knocked on the door and entered. It was one big, empty room with holes in the ceiling and walls. The floor was freshly poured concrete, probably less than a week cured. Claudio and Nino were sweeping up in one of the corners.

"Nino!" Salvator said. "What are you doing here?"

"Harassing your father. What else is there in life?"

"He's looking for a place up here, too," Claudio said. "Thinking about shacking up with that Shaw woman."

Salvator looked at Nino. Nino winked. "You guys living together?"

Nino stuck out his lower lip and nodded, once, very slowly, "Thinking about it, anyway," Nino said. "We found a place out in Blue Lake we like. She ain't a hundred percent yet."

"Why doesn't anybody tell me these things?" Salvator said. "You thinking about getting married or something?"

Nino, his lip still stuck out like a five year old's, shook his head. "She ain't interested in marriage," Nino said.

"So what the hell?" Salvator said.

"She's knows a good thing when she sees it," Nino said, patting the remnants of his belly, flexing each bicep. He posed in the exaggerated look of a glamorous male model.

Claudio pinched the bridge of his nose, laughing: "If bullshit was a snowflake, Nino, you'd be a blizzard."

Nino looked right at Claudio and rubbed the inside corner of his left eye with the fully extended middle finger of his left hand. Good to see Nino, Salvator thought.

"This is going to be my new shop," Claudio said, turning towards Salvator. "I'm going to do custom work for people. Start slaughtering again." He pointed to one corner of the room. "Going to build a cold storage over there." To another corner, "Couple sinks and grinders over there." The center of the room, "My blocks." The far wall, "The old counter."

"You still have that?" Then it hit him: "Slaughter? You're going to do that?"

Claudio nodded. "I can teach you if you're still a butcher."

For a very long time Salvator had wanted to slaughter a cow. He'd felt almost hypocritical as a butcher who'd never actually taken the life of the creatures he sliced up every day. For Paulo, who liked to hunt, it was crucial that a man who professed to eat meat kill his own and clean it himself. One of Paulo's friends, the man he hunted with, came from the Onondaga tribe in Western New York. And for that man, Charlie Coyote, hunting was a deeply spiritual practice, where man and beast work in unison to preserve life. Salvator never considered himself a hunter, indeed had never been hunting, but it had always nagged him that he'd never slaughtered a cow. And this was the great paradox of his life: to give life, I must take life, he thought. The light and the dark, Paulo would call it. Now, maybe with his father's help, he could complete his fragmented circle of life. It would be the hardest thing he would ever do, looking into the eyes of a steer and asking that steer to pass its life to him. But if his father was there with him, and Nino and Paulo, and maybe even Charlie Coyote.

"Got the counter out in the shed on the other side of the house," Claudio said.

Nino handed Salvator his broom. "I gotta take a leak."

Claudio pointed to the rafters with the handle of his broom. "I need to get up there and brush out all those cobwebs," he said. "And fix that roof before the end of this summer."

Salvator stuck out his lower lip and nodded. He took the broom and walked over to the far corner of the room. "This window open?" he said.

"Yes," Claudio said. Claudio took up another broom that was leaning against the wall and started sweeping.

Salvator slid the window open. A slight cross breeze blew through room. He started sweeping in that corner of the room, slowly working his way down along the wall, forming a long pile of debris at the room's edge. Claudio leaned his broom back up against the wall, said, "Gonna go get some lemonade," and left the shack. Salvator continued sweeping the dirt and dust until he'd piled it up in front of the open door. He stood there, in the doorway, his nostrils filled with dust, watching as Claudio, parting the now-thinning fog with his thick frame, exited the house with a big thermos, his head tilted down and bobbing slightly, as if he were nodding agreement to himself. Salvator, standing there in the doorway of the shack, gripped his broom, closed his eyes and thought of Anna's hair

illumino d'immenso

light of immensity

then swept the remaining particles of dust and earth out into the cool, afternoon air.

THE END

About the Author

Vincent Cardinale was born and raised in Oakland, California. He now lives and works in Western New York.

Printed in the United States
23930LVS00003B/334-369